PRAISE FOR RUNAWAY TRAIN

"An engaging '90s pastiche with an earnest heart beating at its center."
—*Kirkus Reviews*

"Raw. Riveting. *Runaway Train* stays true to its title as it explores the deep pain of a teenager desperately trying to find peace in a world full of pain. Lee Matthew Goldberg is a master at bestowing sympathy and strength on deeply flawed characters. Realistic and shocking, hopeful and satisfying, *Runaway Train* will keep readers turning the page."
—*USA Today* Bestselling Author Rebecca Forster

"It's an incredibly challenging task for an author to utilize a darkly comedic tone without coming across as disingenuous—but Goldberg executes it here with expert precision. Brimming over with the visceral atmosphere of the early 90s grunge era, *Runaway Train* is a must-read for those willing to buckle up for the ride."
—Peter Malone Elliott, Book Pipeline

"In *Runaway Train*, Nico takes the leap every teenager dreams of taking, but it's a leap few writers have handled as well as Goldberg. He pulls apart the teen puzzle of feeling both adrift and intentional in the same moment and reminds us that finding a way to be heard is the only way anybody finds themselves."
—Rick Polito, forthcoming author of *Off Trail*

"All fans of '90s alternative, no matter their generation, will find something to love in this book. A story of a young, drifting woman, who has lost her older sister abruptly and decides, as her family crumbles, to run away, *Runaway Train* presents an adventure, an escape fantasy, and the possibilities of life when you're young and on the margins. This book is a delight for readers of all ages."

—Alex DiFrancesco, author of
All City and *Transmutation: Stories*

"*Runaway Train* is a high-energy testimonial to the redemptive power of a road trip with an awesome soundtrack. Lee Matthew Goldberg balances the urgency of youth with a whiff of anticipatory nostalgia for the music and misadventures of late adolescence. Attuned to way distinctions between music genres and teen idols can feel like impermeable walls worth defending, and then crumble as a teen like Nico Sullivan finds her own voice."

— Jenn Stroud Rossman, author of
The Place You're Supposed to Laugh

GRENADE BOUQUETS

A RUNAWAY TRAIN NOVEL

• • • • • • • •

GRENADE BOUQUETS

· · · · · · · ·

LEE MATTHEW GOLDBERG

wisewolfbooks.com

WISE WOLF BOOKS · LAS VEGAS

WISE WOLF
BOOKS

This is a work of fiction. All of the characters, organizations,
publications, and events portrayed in this novel are either products
of the author's imagination or are used fictitiously.

For information, address Wolfpack Publishing,
5130 S. Fort Apache Road, 215-380 Las Vegas, NV 89148

wisewolfbooks.com

Cover design by Wise Wolf Books

Paperback ISBN 978-1-953944-07-8
eBook ISBN 978-1-953944-51-1
LCCN: 2021941178

First Edition: August 2021

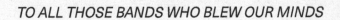

TO ALL THOSE BANDS WHO BLEW OUR MINDS

We are the music makers,
And we are the dreamers of dreams,
Wandering by lone sea-breakers,
And sitting by desolate streams; —
World-losers and world-forsakers,
On whom the pale moon gleams:
Yet we are the movers and shakers
Of the world for ever, it seems.

Arthur O' Shaughnessy "Ode"

SIDE *A*

• • • • •

1994

INTRO

● ● ● ● ● ●

Sick of Myself – Matthew Sweet

I'm barefoot on a roof deck, maybe it's my own, I dunno. Life has been a series of tour buses and motels recently, but I think this is that place the band rented down on the Lower East Side. Everyone hates me and I'm left alone in a huge railroad apartment with a fire escape that twists up to a roof and barely any railing to keep me safe. I have a joint in one hand that's surprisingly still lit in the rain and a trusty bottle of Absolut Citron in the other. I'm wearing a baby doll pale blue dress, the one I rocked during the Grenade Bouquets set when the A&R manager said he was gonna make us stars. I once heard that when you're looking at stars in the sky, you're already looking at the past and they're already dead. I'm seventeen and I can completely relate. I'm over myself and have been looking into the past so much, I might as well be dead.

I chug from the bottle, the excess liquid spilling down my cheeks like hot tears. What lands in my throat, burns and my eye twitches...I'm so bombed.

My makeup has run all over my face and made me into a clown. I pity whoever will find my ghastly remains. I bring the joint to my lips and suck as the cherry flares, the smoke streaming through my nostrils. I'm a dragon in pursuit. Three stories down below, a sea of umbrellas await. I think of Kristen.

Her spirit no longer visits and I understand. She has better things to do than deal with the living. My sister has been gone now for over a year, and sometimes I forget the sound of her voice. I wake up in the middle of the night frantic that I've lost it, and then a glimmer reappears—a whisper in her high pitch calling me back to sleep, aware of how my insomnia can plague me. She would be so proud of my success as a singer and for me to live my dream, not realizing that it was killing me as well. I don't remember the last time I went to bed sober. I feel distant from everyone I used to care about. Evan can't even look at me anymore. I'm Nico the Beast, a whirlwind intent to destroy.

If you heard me on the radio, you'd be jealous. I'm that girl you wish you could be. My song like a spit in the face, a baby Courtney Love with scabbed knees, dark red lipstick, hair dyed so much it's fried, a scowl for a smile. And then in the next song, I'm scrubbed clean, my dress full of flowers rather than ripped, my bruises bandaged, my makeup a light touch rather than an onslaught, singing about love and hope and everything that grunge is not. Because grunge is dying. Kurt Cobain solidified its end and the record companies can smell it. A future of sugary happy pop awaits. What will they do with me, with any of us? We're already that dying star. Might as well help give them a push.

The rain has risen in tempo, a drumbeat on my skull. The joint has gone out and I toss it into the crowd. It disappears into the ether, like I will soon. I picture my obituary, the phrase 'One Hit Wonder' highlighted. All I'll ever be. But I don't have any more songs in me. My quill is broken, my heart has followed—I'm sick of myself.

I raise my arms like Brandon Lee in *The Crow*. Evan and I saw that at the Angelika, an artsy movie theater down on Houston St., which I mispronounced like it was the city Houston. We toured Manhattan that day, the first time either of us had been: hand in hand through The Met and wandering down paths in Central Park, sneaking through the Plaza and pretending I was Eloise, hot chocolates at a place called Serendipity, his blue eyes never letting me out of his sight. I never imagined I could be so in love. Only a short time ago but might as well be a lifetime, those blues will never look at me in the same way again. I'm tarnished, I'm filth. I heard a song called "Only Happy When It Rains", and it couldn't be truer. Miserable people feed off misery and that's all I have to give.

I wonder what my mom and dad will say when they have to identify my body. They've both found new lives with new loves that will be a shoulder for them. Maybe they'll be relieved. Back home, my friend Winter has her own shit to deal with and brought Jeremy into her drama, so they'll mourn but are preoccupied enough to only think of me in passing. I know that's what they do now. They are still in high school and I've dropped out, promising my folks I'd get my GED, but I never did. And high school seems so pointless and far away. I've lived in the real world. I've skipped down New York City streets with crack vials crunching under my feet. Out of spite I've let a man inside of me whose name I didn't even know. I've crowd surfed over a hundred bodies chanting my name. I thought I was in love and never want the pain of it ending ever again. I'd rather be numb. I'd rather be gone.

My feet are cold against the tar of the roof, the toenail polish chipped and starting to fade. I give another swig until the bottle is empty. I aim to launch it into the sky, not caring who I'd hit down below. I climb onto the edge, wobbling, teeth chattering, knees knocking, singing a Matthew Sweet song to the world, to this dark city where I never belonged, so far from a home.

"*But I'm sick of myself when I look at you, something is beautiful and true. World that's ugly and a lie, it's hard to even want to try.*"

My vocal cords are raw from the vodka and pot, my tears make everything blurry. I go to pitch the bottle and my foot slips from a slick of water. I lose my heart as it leaps out of my throat and I think I've gone over the edge, plummeting headfirst to my death. But I fall backwards, smacking my head on the tar. The grey clouds above go in and out of focus until they disappear entirely. My eyes have shut but I can see the night sky, and one little star, so dead but so bright, guiding me not to slip into unconsciousness, praying for my survival. Like a diamond it glows brighter, and I think that maybe it's Kristen's eye, somewhere up in heaven, winking at me to stay on Earth for a little longer because I haven't finished all I intended to do, as the rain washes me pure, its drumbeat now playing Letters to Cleo's beautiful, simmering song, "Here and Now", while I travel back to what led me to become these twisted remains once called a girl.

1

• • • • •

Here and Now – Letters to Cleo

I'm leaving for Vegas tomorrow to join the Grenade Bouquets on their tour. Since it's summer, the 'rents have okayed the trip, as long as I promised to check in with them at every stop. I have to admit that they've been cool. I think they realize I finally found something I'm into and don't want me falling to pieces again. Like when I took off on my runaway extravaganza to mourn my sister's death and went on a series of adventures that led me to meet Evan and the rest of the Bouquets and sing for the first time to Cobain's music at a show. But also, how I'm not as sad and messed up as I used to be before I left.

With both Mom and Dad in new relationships, they are way happier too, and have also made time to talk with me about Kristen. There's a guilty feeling when someone dies that you're not honoring their memory if you don't think about them all the time. It's why I visit Kristen's grave before I jet. I want to take her on this tour with me, but not for every moment. I don't need her ghost like I used to. I've also heard that the dead stick around for a while somewhere between Earth and the afterlife and then follow their path when they're certain their loved ones are ready to let them go. I'm not sure how much I believe this, but I know I'm more ready than I used to be and that's fuckin' progress.

I head over to Winter's for one last hang before my departure. Jeremy is gonna be there too and they want to get bombed. I don't wanna be hungover, but I promised I'd smoke and drink a little, enough to relax. Last minute, Winter let me know that her new stupid friend Emily, who I refer to as Emily Valentine—the *90210* psycho—would be hanging out too. On *90210*, Emily Valentine was a bad influence on Brandon by making him do euphoria, a completely made-up drug that was likely closest to ecstasy, and she did a ton of other sketchy shit too. I don't see this Emily being any different. She's sidled up to Winter and now they're joined at the hip because Winter needs that in a friendship. While I don't want it to bother me so much, it does. Winter has been my ride or die since we were eleven, and it's weird to see someone else besides Jeremy sharing her clothes. I try to tell myself that I'm moving on to bigger and better things with the Grenade Bouquets, but Winter has a way of making herself the focus and she always will.

Winter's mom Edina opens the door after one knock. She has a joint smoking in an old timey cigarette holder and her orange hair is in pigtails that actually look cute.

"Nico," she says, with a light hug. "I heard about your show!" She waves the smoke from my face. "I always said you had a beautiful voice that you should share with the world."

"Thanks," I say, walking inside. Scott McKenzie's "San Francisco" plays from a record.

"I hear you're going on tour with a band too." Edina makes a face like she knows the kind of trouble I'm about to get into and wags her finger. She sings along with the song. "Be sure to wear, some flowers in your hair."

She plucks a daisy from a vase and places it behind my ear. "I'm so proud."

"I'm excited," I say, and burp. "And nervous."

In fact, my stomach's been giving me hell ever since Evan asked me to go. For a second, I even wondered if I was pregnant but then remembered that Evan and I hadn't actually slept together yet.

"Nerves are good," she says, and then directs her hands over me without touching. "I've been practicing reiki. I'm feeding you energy right now. Good energy." She smiles and shows off a few twisted teeth before planting the roach between her lips and feeding me more good energy. I don't feel nothing, but nod like I do because Edina is a true empath and only wants the best for people.

"You're gonna be a firecracker," she says, in her posh British accent. "And I can say I once knew you when."

She shudders in delight and sings her way toward the kitchen. I turn and brace myself for Winter's room. It's been a little weird between us this summer. I'd been working in the record store and busy with singing lessons, and it seemed like all Winter did was get plastered with loser Emily Valentine. Jeremy even said that Emily did some harder stuff, but he wasn't specific and didn't say if Winter experimented too. It's one thing to have some pot and a drink as long as you kept it to a limit, but another to go harder. It makes me think of that one pill I took in Seattle and how I wound up in the hospital. We knew kids at school that did coke, and they always acted like totally different people when high, vicious and mean. Emily used to roll with those guys, so I wouldn't be too surprised if she still did and brought Winter along.

To document my trip, I decided to make a mixtape. The last time I made one was for Kristen, but this one would be for me. The first song I dubbed was Letters to Cleo's, "Here and Now", kinda a sweeter sound than some of my other favorite bands. Maybe it's just because I've been in a sweeter mood than I used to be. Anyway, I recorded the song and figured I'd gift Winter with the CD from the store I worked at. I had them wrap it up all nice with a tiny card.

I knock on the door as I enter and Winter, Jeremy, and stupid Emily Valentine are sitting on Winter's bed cross-legged and immediately stop talking, which means they were probably talking about me. I realize Winter has completely changed the décor since it's no longer a shrine to Eddie Vedder and Pearl Jam. The posters have been taken down and replaced with Marilyn Manson, who has songs like "Cake and Sodomy", "Organ Grinder", "Wrapped in Plastic", and is, honestly, like too much for me. He's just gross and shocks for shock-sake so I find him phony. But Winter obviously has a new idol. Marilyn Manson stares back at me from every wall with his ghostly face and stringy hair, what looks like blood for lipstick, and one eye entirely white. Winter and Emily have already aped his look, both recently dying their hair jet black and leaving it unwashed and long. They wear matching leather tops that show off their belly buttons, chokers so tight it cuts off their circulation, and white makeup on their face with blood-red lips. They look like death warmed over.

"Oh, hey, Nico," Jeremy says, bubbly and bouncing his way over with a kiss on my cheek. "We were just talking about trying to make ourselves faint."

My voice gets trapped in a burp I try to squelch down. "Faint?"

"Like, I've done it," Emily Valentine says, flipping her hair back like she's the king of shit. And then she and Winter give a smoker's laugh that makes my skin crawl. "You target pressure points and then just go unconscious."

"Cool."

"What's that?" Winter asks, pointing at my gift with a sharp fingernail.

"Oh, it's for you." I pass over the present, which Winter coolly opens like she doesn't really give a crap.

"Letters to Cleo?" she asks, holding it like a dirty diaper.

Emily Valentine sticks her tongue into her cheek and shakes her head.

"Thanks," Winter says, shrugging her shoulders and chucking it on the bed.

"I'm making a mixtape for my tour and that's gonna be the first song, so I figured I'd give you the album."

Emily Valentine goes to whisper in Winter's ear like the slithery eel she is.

"What?" I say, as threatening as possible.

"It's just…" Emily Valentine gives a dark smile, her teeth so white amongst the red lipstick. "We're like Marilyn Manson loyalists now, so…"

"So, we're only listening to him," Winter continues. "It's like a pact."

"Okay." I swipe the CD and hand it over to Jeremy. "Jeremy, you enjoy it."

Jeremy looks like he has no idea what to do, his eyes shifting from me to Winter and down to his old Reebok Pumps.

"Jeremy, keep it," Winter says, like a wise old sage. "It's more your style. Ya-know, poppy." Then Winter and Emily share in a fit of giggles.

I'm stewing and I want to punch Emily Valentine in her dumb choker and then slap Winter across her too-white makeup'd face, but I give a *woosah* like my Aunt Carly taught me to do and kill 'em with kindness. Aunt Carly had been a godsend when I was going through the worst of it, living up in Ojai with her crystals and chill attitude. She was the one who first supported my decision to find myself and got me on the path of my wild journey. I'll be forever indebted to her.

"So, I leave tomorrow," I say, chewing on a finger-nail. "Vegas is my first stop."

"It's for Nico's band," Jeremy says to Emily.

"Well, it's not my band," I say, even though it tickles me to hear about it spoken that way. *My* band. "But I'll be guest singing on a few songs."

"With your hot boyfriend playing back-up guitar,"

Jeremy says.

I think of Evan. His blond hair messy and covering his eyes. A striped-green sweater he'd swim in, lean muscles and a spritz of Cool Water cologne, even though he'd never admit it.

"We haven't seen each other over much of the summer, so we'll see what–"

"What's his dick like?" Emily blurts out, and Winter swats at her but they are laughing, this cruel giggle they have between them that I'm not a part of.

"We haven't, I mean, we're waiting... We haven't done it yet."

This gets the two hyenas going even worse.

"You can't call someone your *boy*friend if you haven't even done it," Emily declares. She unravels from her Lotus position on the bed and walks over to Winter's desk where there are a few bottles of alcohol. She goes down the line and samples each one. I make a face.

"What?" Winter asks, leaping up.

"What?" I say, fixing my face.

"You were giving Emily the stink eye."

"She just mixed a shot of rum, vodka, and that peach liquor you love."

"So, Emily is a trailblazer," Winter says, as Emily gives a drunken "Yeah!"

Emily is licking her gums now, and I wonder if the two of them are acting so vicious because they've done something harder before I opened the door.

"Anyway, I have an early flight so I just wanted to say goodbye."

"Bye bye," Emily says, dancing with a bottle. She

turns Winter's stereo up and horrible Marilyn Manson screeches from the speakers. Winter mewls along.

"They're just loaded," Jeremy says into my ear, low enough so the two dumb alley cats can't hear.

"Like, she knows how nervous I am about going," I say, fighting back a tear. But I don't want to cry for Winter, not anymore.

"She has a hard time saying goodbye."

"She's a baby," I say, and give Jeremy a squeezing hug. I brush his frosted bang tips from out of his eyes. He's truly my best friend, never judging, always caring. "I'm gonna miss you."

"You're gonna be amazing, Nico." And then under his breath. "They're jealous."

I look up and Winter is cutting me with her eyes. She's dancing with stupid Emily Valentine, but not paying any attention to her. Every fiber in her being is directed toward me. I see sadness staring back because we both know that once I leave, nothing will ever be the same between us again. I would keep leaving, time after time, whether it's with the Grenade Bouquets or another band, this was my future. And she exudes rottenness because she knows she doesn't have a future. I'm living in the here and now, ready for whatever awaits. She's stuck in this dank room with a hanger-on who she probably hates and fresh new cuts along her arms and thighs because of how much she hates herself.

I want to hug her. I want to tell her that for so long it was us against the world and it can still be, but I'm chicken. I know she'll reject me, even though she totally wants us back to how we used to be. Our pride greater than our love. She licks her gums and gives up staring me down as I hunch my shoulders and slip out of the door.

Edina glides by with her caftan billowing and "Turn! Turn! Turn!" by the Byrds playing from a new record, as she asks me why I'm "leaving so soon"? I want to cry into her shoulder, but I bite down on my lip to stop the tears overflowing and say, "I need to rest my vocal cords," like I'm goddamn Barbara Streisand before a show at Radio City Music Hall. She passes me a lozenge from her pocket, even though we both know I don't need it, even though we silently understand how cruel her daughter can be, and that I no longer have room in my life to take that abuse. She gives a nod, showing that she doesn't blame me and whispers, "Nico, never look back," before humming along to the record.

So, I do as well, "*To everything turn, turn, turn!*"

2

• • • • • •

Genetic – Sonic Youth

When I get home, Mom is on the couch with one of those huge mugs that could be used for soup or tea. She's got the AC blasting and wearing a sweater with wool scrunchie socks like a loon. I'm surprised not to see Mr. Ferguson, or rather, Roger, her new boyfriend. Most nights they sit on the couch together and watch old romantic films like *Roman Holiday* or *Bringing Up Baby*. Old movies bug me, the acting seems so forced and fake, and everything is so overdramatic. I'd rather watch *Heathers* for the nineteen-thousandth time. Mom and Roger have a pretty sweet setup. Roger literally lives next door with only a fence separating them, so they haven't moved in together yet. They decided to ix-nay the idea of putting an extension between their houses. Something I'm not ready for either, since Roger has two chow-chows that take giant log-like shits that would make even the Log Lady from *Twin Peaks* proud.

"Nico," Mom says, as she waves me over. She

removes a knitted blanket from the seat next to her and pats for me to sit. I curl up and see she's watching *My So-Called Life.*

"Aren't you a little old for that show?" I ask, as I watch Angela make moon eyes for Jordan Catalano.

"I *was* once in high school too, ya-know," she says, and her eyes glaze over. I imagine she's remembering times from the olden days. "Although it was so different than what you kids are dealing with now. Alcoholism, school violence, AIDS…"

I have a realization that my high-school life has basically been *My So-Called Life* and not *90210.* I'm Angela, Winter's wild Rayanne, and Jeremy is flamboyant Rickie. Although there'd never been a boy like Jordan Catalano in the halls who looked my way.

Mom wraps an errant hair around my ear and fingers my faux diamond stud. "How was Winter's?"

I must've made a *harumph* sound because she gets this concerned dent between her eyes.

"I dunno…" I try to form what I want to say. "Winter can be such a bitch."

Mom mutes the TV as Claire Danes with her crimson hair flails around in her oversized flannel at a backyard party before she gets shoved in the mud.

"It's probably hard for her to watch you go."

"I'm only like going for a few weeks."

"Sweetie, you two aren't glued at the hip anymore, it's natural."

I pick up her big mug and take a sip. It's ginger tea. "Really?"

"Not everyone gets a best friend in high school like

you both had. But you can't stay best friends forever, it's not possible. There'll be college and jobs and husbands and many new friends. I haven't talked to my best friend Lucille in ages."

"Isn't she the one who sells hair?"

"It's for a non-profit charity, but yes, she does sell hair for wigs. That's my point. We're so different. She never had children…" Mom pauses at the word 'children' and then recalibrates, her hardwire telling her she only has one child now. A sigh like a fog over a moor escapes from her lips. "We grew apart. Like what's happening with Angela and Rayanne," she continues, nodding at the TV. "And with you and Winter."

"She has this godawful new friend Emily, who's like the worst. And I think they…" I struggle to say they might be doing cocaine. Mom might think she's all cool with her *My So-Called Life* knowledge, but cocaine would be too big a leap. "She's a bad influence."

Mom pulls me close. We used to do this when I was little, snuggle up and eat a bowl of Teddy Grahams or something. But then I became a demon around the age of eleven and shut myself up in my room blaring Nirvana whenever I was home.

"My baby's singing in a band," Mom says, wistfully to herself as she unmutes the TV and "Genetic" by Sonic Youth plays over Angela's troubles. Mom moves to the music like she's trying to be cool, and it's hella whack, but actually cute at the same time. "Promise me you'll make safe choices when you're on the road."

"Mom, it's not like I haven't been on my own before." I'm referring to my runaway escapades from last spring, and she gives me a look that tells me it's *too soon* to make jokes like that.

"Your father is going to pick you up first thing in the morning to take you to the airport."

"Did I tell you how hella great you guys are for letting me go?"

Her lips form a flat line. "Did we have a choice?"

I inspect a fried split hair of mine that's a mix of blue and lavender. "No."

"I was the same when I was your age. Burned my bra instead of going on tour with a band. Never colored in the lines. My mother couldn't stand that."

I picture her burning her bra with her tits swinging strong and wild in a 1960's wind.

"I didn't know you burned your bra, like a hippie?"

"Someday, Nico, I'll tell you stories." She taps my knee. "But you should head to bed now. You know how your father is about being on time." She gags when she says, my 'father', the contempt between the two of them still apparent, although they've tried to be so good around me and co-parent civilly. Mom even invited Dad's new paramour Annette over for dinner a few weeks ago and made a casserole.

"I love you," she says. "More than I love anyone."

"I know."

She releases me from a strangling hug with a tea-filled kiss and goes back to watching *My So-Called Life*. Now Angela is home drenched in mud, and her mom with the new short haircut puts on her concerned-face.

I skip up the stairs, singing "Genetic" under my breath, and set my alarm for five a.m. I get into bed, but I'm wide-awake, imagining myself singing the song before a screaming crowd while Evan and the rest of Grenade Bouquets shred behind me. They are chanting, "Nico, Nico."

I go to sleep with my name being echoed.

***

At five-thirty on the dot, Dad is already honking outside of the house and my hair is still wet from the shower and I'm dragging my suitcase down the stairs. I packed as light as possible with only one suitcase and a backpack for the next few weeks. Evan said that's all that could fit in the van and we'd be spending our money at laundromats, or wouldn't wash our stuff at all, which I'm cool with.

Inside the car, Annette is fixing her "Rachel" hairdo in the rearview while putting rouge on her cheeks. "Upwards," she always told me, "you always want to brush upwards." I want to say I'll remember that when I turn middle-age, but I try to be nice.

"You ready, Scrap?" Dad asks, looking at me through his new bifocals. He's begun dyeing his hair since he met Annette, but the silver-grey still peeks through in fits and spurts.

"Ready Freddy," I say, as we shoot down I-405 to LAX. This early hour is the one of the few times there's barely any cars on the road. I'm able to roll down the window and stick my hand out and make it dance with the breeze.

At the airport in the departures section, Dad fumbles in his pockets until he whips out a gas card.

"I'll be monitoring this, so don't overspend," he

says, and we do a tug of war with the card like he's regretting handing it over. Finally, he lets go. "Okay, rules," he says, and Annette rubs his back in swirling motions to calm him down. "One, no drugs. At these concerts, many people will try to offer you drugs, and you must say no. Also, never take a drink from someone else because it might be roofied." He pushes up the glasses on his beak nose. I think of how Winter would always refer to him as Richard Gere from *Pretty Woman*, and I fight with everything in me not to vom. "You are to call when you reach each city on the tour, both to me and your mom, because she worries; I mean she'll be in my ear if you don't."

Annette shakes her head like *isn't my mom such a crazy lady?*

"And boys," he says, his eyes magnifying behind his glasses. "This boy you've been with...the one in the band...you need to make sure...that if...well, if you two decide to be intimate..."

"Dad!"

My cheeks turn red enough to look like Annette went nuts with the rouge on them.

"Peter," Annette says, jumping in to bring him back to some kind of sanity. "She's a good girl."

"Yeah, I am, like I'm gonna be responsible. I have too much on my mind with singing to screw it all up."

Dad grimaces, clearly not fully trusting me yet after I ran away, but part of him is probably afraid that if they said no to this excursion, I might run away for good. Even though I wouldn't—I mean, I don't think so. Who knows what I'd do if they kept me from my dream?

"Just…be well," he says, with a side-hug, the most kind of warmth I'd get from him, but that's okay. It's Dad being Dad.

"Bye, darling," Annette says, with three kisses back and forth on my cheeks. And then they are waving and getting smaller as I drag my suitcase to the check-in desk. After I get my ticket, I expect them to still be waving but they're gone and I have this creeping churning sensation in my stomach that I'm all alone. I have my journey's mixtape loaded in my Sports Walkman, so I put on my headphones and hit play and escape into the music as I wait for my flight to board.

Vegas, baby, here I come.

3

Bizarre Love Triangle – Frente!

The flight to Vegas from L.A. is basically up then down, barely any time for me to have more than an o.j. I'd never flown solo before and the stewardess is super nice and makes sure I'm getting picked up by someone when I arrive. "Yeah, my band will," I say, casually with a flip of my hair like it's no big deal, and her eyebrows rise with respect. I feel more adult in that moment than I ever have before. She gives me an extra bag of peanuts.

I'm munching on the peanuts while dragging my suitcase from the arrivals when I see Evan, all lean with his hair styled in a messy swoop across one eye and a fuzzy sweater with holes. A peanut nearly gets trapped in my throat and I hack as he notices and I'm all red in the face by the time I reach him.

"Rogue peanut," I say, pointing at my throat but he scoops me up with a big swirling hug and we are THAT COUPLE kissing in the airport like we've been apart for eons. He tastes like spearmint Chewels gum with the spurt of goo in the middle.

"How was your flight?" he asks, as we walk holding hands out of the airport.

"It's so good to see you." His hand is clammy and I think that's cute because he's nervous like I am. We're entering a new stage of our relationship after being apart for months with only one visit when he came to L.A. I feel like I want to declare my love for him but stop my stupid ass from being embarrassing. I repeat to *stay cool, keep cool*, over and over in my head until it's mantra.

"It's good to see you too, Nico." He smiles, and I relax. Part of me worried he might've regretted inviting me along to sing, but I know that's only me jinxing myself. I'm worthy. "The Bouquets are parked in the lot with our van."

Our van is a broken-down VW that's fire-engine red on the bottom and white on top with five windows on each side and tiny bubble windows by the ceiling. It's rusted and gnarly and perfect. Ed and Randy wait outside of it, Randy playing air drums against Ed's back. Clarissa smokes a 100 cigarette, hand on her hip, while talking with Lacey, our band manager.

"Nico," they all cheer in a way that warms my heart. Well, maybe Clarissa didn't cheer because she used to date Evan and can't be too jazzed I've arrived, but everyone else seems genuinely happy to see me.

Ed gives a big hug being a big guy, his arms squeezing like a bear. Randy, the oldest of the group, and likely around thirty, is less exuberant with a hug but still says he's glad to see me. I missed the two of them, imagining how I'd come to think of both as older brothers looking out for me on tour.

"Nico," Lacey says, pulling me into her embrace. She runs her fingers through my hair. "Love the blue dye job. Manic Panic?"

"You know it."

Lacey always looks so cool in her vintage get-ups: librarian glasses with a Sally Jessy Raphael vibe, a bob haircut, and a polka dot dress buttoned-up to her neck with saddle shoes.

"Hi, Clarissa," I say, because she's the only one who hasn't approached me yet. She's shaved the right side of her head with the left kept long like Ani Di-Franco. Raccoon eyes and dark, dark lip liner, and a D.A.R.E. to Keep Kids Off Drugs tee under a leopard strappy dress. And Doc Martins; we're all wearing Doc Martins.

"Hi," she says, exhaling smoke and stamping the cigarette out under her boot. No hug, but I didn't expect one.

"This could be our album cover," Evan says, smiling through the awkwardness of the situation and snapping a pretend picture as we all pose.

"Wait, I'll take a picture for real," Lacey says, and rummages in her purse for a camera. We all pose again: Ed giving a roar, Randy getting close to Evan, Evan flipping his bangs out of his eyes, Clarissa looking bored and unaffected, and me squelching a burp. The sun is hot and boiling and glimmering off of the VW and I wonder if we'll look back on this years later if we're all still together and think of how young and hopeful we were.

***

In the van, Ed drives with Randy sitting shotgun while Evan and I sit in the backseat with Lacey and Clarissa in front of us. Ed is searching the radio stations but can't find any he likes so I offer up my mixtape and "Bizarre Love Triangle" by Frente! comes on. It's a sweeter version than the New Order original, the lead singer's voice like syrup.

"Haven't heard this before," Evan says.

"Yeah, I've been exploring some new bands, mostly female singer led ones. My voice teacher–"

Clarissa whips her head around. "You're only singing on two songs, you know." Her raccoon eyes sear into my soul.

"Yeah, I know that," I say, trying to sound tough but I imagine it comes off more like a chipmunk.

"Clarissa," Evan says, in an admonishing tone she can't be too happy to hear. I see a window into their former relationship: Clarissa being difficult and Evan schooling her like he should.

"I'm just setting parameters," she says, and looks to Lacey to defend. "Like, so she knows her place. Nico," she continues, "I'm ever so grateful that you helped the Bouquets out while I was in Italy, but just be aware that you're the *back*-up singer for this tour and we'll be fine."

I can smell my pits because I'm sweating and the van doesn't have any AC. "I never said I wasn't."

I feel Evan reach to take my hand, but mine is sopping wet so I don't comply.

"Good," she chirps. "It's important that we all understand our roles. There's a lot of pressure on me as the lead singer..." She says this puckering her lips into a compact before snapping it shut. "I'm sure you understand."

I stick my tongue into my cheek and imagine her head in a guillotine.

"Hey," Evan says, touching her shoulder. "Relax." And I'm like, why are you touching this ho bag's shoulder while she bats her eyelashes? I stick my hands under my butt to avoid choking her head off. "Nico was so great when she sang with us, and she's really doing a favor by joining the tour."

"I know," Clarissa laughs, a cackle from a devil. "I'm kidding." She swats at the air. "Nico knows I'm kidding, don't you, Nico?" I'm silent. "It's like a hazing ritual."

Evan starts quietly laughing along too. "Oh, okay, yeah she's just kidding, Nico."

He's looking at me with his sea-blue eyes like, *please don't make a big deal of this*. And since I can be the bigger person, I give a chuckle too.

"Yeah, I knew that."

Now Lacey laughs along, but I can tell she was concerned. We eye each other, and in the moment, I know she has my back against the vixen that is Clarissa.

"Like, we all need to lighten up," Clarissa says, taking out a pack of her 100 cigarettes and lighting up. "You want one, Nico?"

I'm not a smoker. Honestly, if I'm gonna destroy my lungs let it be from weed, so I at least get a buzz out of it. But I slide a cigarette from her pack that she lights. I don't like the way she's looking at me, as if she has the ability to throw my emotions into a tizzy any time she wants, the clever little minx.

I feel Evan reach to take my hand again, and I let him this time. I'm perspiring less, and I want Clarissa to see how much Evan and I are a unit. I take a puff and ease into his armpit, cuddling with my man. I puff and cuddle, puff and cuddle, knowing it's making her go berserk. She puffs away too, but one of her eyes is twitching like mad, fluttering like a hummingbird's wing. I torture her more by giving Evan a kiss on his stubbly cheek. And then I laugh too, like a madwoman who's not here to play around, no longer the wet-behind-the-ears high school girl anyone can mess with. I direct my exhale of smoke right toward her smug face and then apologize, but in a way like I'm not really apologizing, like I did it on purpose, and the apology just rubs it in even more.

Her twitching eye goes into overdrive as the Frente! song ends.

4

●　●　●　●　●

Violet – Hole

We're playing at a venue called Elvis' Last Toilet off of the Strip in Spring Valley, a scuzzy bar full of King tchotchkes and beer-scented floors. It's hot and everything's flat and the casinos are all two miles away in the smog. I have zero interest in gambling so I don't mind not going. We'll be able to do a run-through before the show tonight. I'm singing on Hole's "Violet" with Clarissa and then solo for my stripped-down version of Ace of Base's "The Sign", a nod to Kristen because that was her favorite song. Honestly, it's been growing on me too. We set everything up and the band launches into "Disarm" by the Smashing Pumpkins with Evan singing and on guitar. He thinks he doesn't have the best voice, but it's really sublime. It has a nasally similarity to Billy Corgan's and Cobain as well, but more vulnerable, like it could shatter at any moment. I'm the only member in the audience and he's singing right to me. Clarissa harmonizes during the chorus, clearly unhappy that I'm his focus.

The band plays Evan's original song next, the one about his brother who came home from Iraq with mental issues. I can see how difficult it is for Evan, his voice going wobbly at times, but he powers through. I mouth to him that he's doing great. A tiny smirk creeps up his cheek, like he wants to smile but doesn't wanna appear uncool, so he tempers it down. They play "In Bloom" next, Evan and Randy thrashing back-to-back, before finishing up with the Lemonheads' "Into Your Arms", Evan and Clarissa both on vocals, complementing each other well. But while Evan has stage presence—you can't *not* look at him—Clarissa seems like she's *trying* to have stage presence. She's hitting all the right notes, but her movements are choreographed like she practiced them in the mirror. I vow to move my body at random once I'm on stage. Clear my mind and go into a zone where the music is all that exists. So, I can transcend.

"You're up, Nico," Evan says, after they've finished. He extends a hand and pulls me up on stage. We decide we'll do the same during the show. I can hype the crowd, get a mosh pit going, and then for our finale, jump up and join.

***

I'm happy with how the set goes. I hold my own with Clarissa singing "Violet", and my version of "The Sign" is good, but I know it could be better. The nerves kicked in, part of it having to do with no audience to pump me up. It's also wiser to be more subdued during the rehearsal and wow 'em for the actual show.

I'm in the bathroom fixing my white baby doll dress with tulle like Courtney Love wears in the "Violet" video. Ever since Cobain died, I've become more drawn to her. I used to be jealous, but now I find us soul sisters. We've both suffered loss and are coming out stronger because of it. Hole is bigger than they ever were when Cobain was alive. All summer I've been hearing "Miss World" on the radio. They say that the best art sometimes comes from the worst of times, which Courtney Love and I could attest.

I'm getting the makeup and hair right. I want a look with my hair like I just rolled around in bed. My face powdered white with a glam mauve lipstick and a hint of dark eye shadow. I'm clipping a few pink barrettes in my hair of kissable lips when Clarissa smashes inside with a beer in her hand.

She raises her eyebrows hello and that's all I'm getting. She stands in front of the sink, wetting her neck cause it's so damn hot.

"You nervous?" she finally asks, putting on dark lipliner.

"No," I say, because I know that's not what she wants to hear.

"Yes, you are." She gives a Cheshire Cat grin. "You're pissing your pants." She licks her teeth. "Ya-know, when Evan and I were together…"

I grip the sink, fighting to contain myself for fear of where this might go.

"Like we were each other's world. We spent *every* minute together. He couldn't get enough of me."

"Obviously that changed."

"Meow, Nico, kitten's got sharp claws. The two

of us burned too hot, I don't think we could stand it. That's why we broke up. We were consuming one another—it was destroying the band. So, it was a sacrifice of sorts. For the better of the Bouquets."

I'm ignoring her by working on getting my lip barrettes just right.

"Like, you can't have both." She laughs but it sounds like a hack. "The boy and the band. No couples can make it work. One or the other will always go south."

"I heard you cheated on him."

"What?"

"You two didn't end it for the better of the band. You were just easy."

I don't even know the full extent of what happened between them, but her face tells me I've hit a nerve. I shrug a shoulder, poof up the tulle of my dress, and spin around out of the bathroom. It's always good to be the one who gets the last word.

The venue has about twenty-or-so people milling around. We're the opener for this other band Slay Ride, who I never heard of but Ed told me are known in Vegas. A few minutes later, the Bouquets get up on stage and I decide to nurse a beer thanks to my Sasha Lioni fake ID, which never steers me wrong. I don't want to get back in the habit of drinking too much, but one beer is no BFD—Big Fuckin' Deal.

"We're Grenade Bouquets," Clarissa says into the mic, with a put-upon scowl. Such a try-hard. They launch into "Disarm" and the crowd sways along. When they get to "In Bloom", I start thrashing around at the first sign of hard guitars. Two dudes are pushing each other and a beautiful mosh pit is born. Others join and we're getting out our aggression. It's hyping me up to sing. The blood in my veins on fire, more ready than ever. I'm seething as the band moves to Evan's song about his brother. It's angry and he's exposed, the mosh pit more rhythmic than before, like we all understand what everyone needs to get out of this bellicosity. They play "Into My Arms" next, a song you can't mosh to, and I make a note not to toy with the crowd like this, going from a hard to a soft ballad so soon. The crowd's not as into this duet, starting to talk amongst themselves or go to the bar for another drink. I can't tell if it's bothering Evan, he's singing almost with his eyes closed. I'll have to win 'em over with "Violet".

And then my name is called, and a few people clap. I bunch up my dress and leap on stage. There's a version of me falling over and embarrassing myself before it even begins, but not in this reality. I stick my landing like I'm fuckin' Kerry Strug at the Olympics.

"Thank you, Vegas," I say, grabbing the mic. "I'm Nico and this is our twisted version of 'Violet'."

The shredding opening licks kick in, low at first as I sing the opening lyrics about the sky being made of amethysts and the stars being just like little fish before screaming "you should learn how to say no".

Clarissa's singing along with me but I leave her in the dust. I'm a banshee on stage, attacking everything in my path. Out of the corner of my eye, I see her stunned, before I forget her completely. She doesn't exist. This is my song and mine alone. I'm jumping off the stage, I'm moshing with the crowd. I'm wrapping the microphone cord around my body like a tourniquet, leaving my lipstick on the mic. The energy of the pit doubles, triples, *woo hoos* shouted into the air as the song pivots soft as quickly as it got loud. I'm telling everyone that they get what they want, and they never want it again. The guitars power up as I screech to "go on take everything, take everything, I want you to, go on take everything, take everything I dare you to…"

I'm yelling at Winter, who's found a new ride-or-die, I'm yelling at Kristen for taking her fatal run through Laurel Canyon where she dropped dead. I'm spouting at Clarissa for trying to get between me and Evan. I'm screaming at her now, my voice overpowering hers. She's a mouse and I'm a wolf. There's a gash on my arm and blood spotted on my white dress. I face the audience and lick it up good. They're cheering like they haven't done yet since the band started playing. I'm channeling Courtney Love now, singing directly to her husband who left us all by killing himself. I'm still angry with him. But I swear to keep his torch alive.

I end the song with a curtsey and sit cross-legged down on the stage. The crowd loved every minute of it, cheering but still moshing. Evan comes over and shakes his fist in triumph. "You were awesome," he says. No one's congratulating Clarissa. She's a non-entity. Evan takes the mic.

"For our last song, our special guest Nico Sullivan will be singing an alternate version of something you've heard on the radio all fuckin' summer long. But we've made it grungy and moody, and I hope you like. Thanks, we're the Grenade Bouquets."

Evan starts strumming his guitar like it's a Portishead song, dragging Ace of Base's "The Sign" through muddy puddles filled with needles. The mosh pit quietens, the venue dark except for a lone white light on me, turning "The Sign" into pure anguish. I'm singing with tears bubbling under each breath. As I stand, the song opens up with the chorus, and I can tell the audience is in awe. They did not expect this after the shriek of "Violet", but they're going on this journey with me. I have them rapt, snarling the lyrics like they've done me dirty, leaving them on the stage in pools of my spit. When it's over, a shiver gooses my body, a delicious tickle, the room bone quiet, until it erupts in a roar. The sound of their worship, their devotion. I'm hooked. I drop the mic, wipe the blood from my lips, and leap off the stage, stalking away like a mysterious wraith as "Thank you, Veeeeegas," pumps over the speakers.

***

We're at the bar celebrating with fireball shots that burn my throat cinnamon. I need them to settle my nerves and bring my adrenaline level down to a steady heartbeat thump. I don't think or realize how many I've had. They just taste so good, and I'm so on fire right now. Ed and Randy are ripped, reliving playing "Violet" and how much the mosh pit ruled. Even Slay Ride said my singing was killer before they left with groupies in tow. Lacey's gushing and declares that was "our most alive show yet". Evan's got his arms around me, and he smells of Cool Water and sweat. Clarissa's at the end of the bar, nursing a rum and Coke with a long straw, not eager to join in our celebration.

"Get what they want, but they never want it againnnnn," I hear Ed and Randy shout. "Nico, you ruled."

I try not to look bashful. It's not easy hearing accolades because I'm not used to them yet. I'm still that shy girl alone singing in my room, knowing my voice kicks ass but unsure I'll ever share it with the masses.

"I'm really gonna promote our next show," Lacey says, pushing up her glasses to the bridge of her nose. "In fact, lemme leave before I get too wasted. I'm gonna see if we can get a write-up in a magazine."

"Hella cool," I say.

She's chewing her lip. "I mean, you owned that stage, Nico. It was like star presence." She kisses me on the cheek and flutters away.

Evan pulls me close. "You really were that good. I could see how the crowd was reacting before you came on. When you did, it took us to this other level." He soars his hands through the air like a plane. "When I was playing along to your voice, like, we were fused, we were creating this fuckin' art. Man, it's why I do this."

"I did feel like I left my body," I say, holding onto the memory when I wasn't human for three minutes and forty-five seconds.

"Totally, it's what all the greats chase, an enlightenment."

"I think you've had too many fireballs."

He laughs into his arm. "I do feel like I have dragon breath from all the cinnamon."

I look over at Clarissa at the end of the bar and she's far from laughing, practically crying into her drink. She sees the future of the Bouquets and how I'm nudging in, Nico the burrower.

"She threatened me in the bathroom," I say, unable

to resist.

"Huh?" The way Evan's staring at me I can tell he sees two.

"Our relationship. She said we couldn't have *it* and the band, that one would be destroyed. It's what happened with you and her."

He glances over at Clarissa like some vague part of his past he can't locate.

"Yeah, I mean, she and I fought a ton. We would set each other off. So, it was better off."

"She still likes you," I say, because I have to let it be known, whatever the consequences. I wait for his reaction, if he hems and haws meaning he still has feelings for her too.

"No way," he says, shaking his head. "And I don't think of her that way anymore. I've always been like that, once the relationship ends, it's like it never happened." He plays with my fingers. "I'm only into the present, best way to live life. You're my present."

Squee.

I tug on my lip with my fang tooth and we kiss. Clarissa's eyes shift over, stalking. She pushes her stool into the bar and clomps off, brushing past us in an angry wind.

"Dude, she's still into you," I say, as she gives the bathroom door a hard push. "A whiff of her jealousy is still in the air."

"Nah," Evan says, finishing his shot. Now he's swaying, almost falling off his stool.

"Let's get you to the motel."

We've got two rooms down the street at a nearby dump, one for the boys and one for the girls. I take him to the boys' room, lie him on the bed, and take off his Doc Martins. He pulls me closer, his eyes half closed.

"Stay with me tonight," he murmurs.

"You're so drunk," I say.

"Just to sleep, to hold you, Nico. I missed holding you."

Who could say no to that? I get out of my baby doll dress, brush my teeth with mouthwash and climb into bed in my undergarments. He's already asleep, delicately dreaming, and I kiss him on the forehead, my body stuck to his because the hotel doesn't have AC. The instant I fall asleep, Ed and Randy burst in the room, loud and wasted, popping beer cans, and Evan wakes up at their insistence to join. I grab my dress on the floor to cover myself up and go down the hall to my room to where Lacey is already asleep. I think of being with Evan fully when the time is right, not when we're bombed, since we've waited this long. I think of our music fused together on stage, and how we'll only gel even more at every show until the world completely falls away and it's only the two of us. I go to sleep with a dream of us on a tiny island existing with only a palm tree as other company. When I wake, I'm grinning and see that Clarissa never came back here to sleep. I imagine her wandering the strip with hot tears spilling down her devious cheeks.

5

• • • • •

Leaving Las Vegas – Sheryl Crow

The second Bouquets show at Elvis' Last Toilet was
even better than the first. Lacey called in a favor from
a friend of her older sister who worked at a 'zine called
Guitar Picks that showcases new bands in the grunge
scene. I repeated my "Violet" performance like thirty
thousand people were in the stands. There was a slightly bigger crowd who heard about yesterday's show
and wanted to see Slay Ride's final leg of their tour.
Folks even whipped out their lighters when I sang my
version of "The Sign".

The journalist was a guy named Dan Rhodes who
had long hair and lots of stubble. He had to run but
labeled my performance "Right on" and promised a
write-up in Guitar Picks' newest issue that would be
heading to print soon. His assistant even snapped a
picture of us holding guitar picks. I pretended I was
slitting my throat with mine.

Ed and Randy wanted to party afterwards and
Clarissa seemed to disappear with the drummer from

Slay Ride. I grabbed Evan by the sleeve and whispered in his ear that I wanted it to only be me and him tonight. So, we ditched the rest of the crew and toured the Strip.

***

We enter the Excalibur Casino that had been recently built and looks like Disneyworld. We're underage to gamble but our fake IDs get us through. We play blackjack and roulette and lose. There are showgirls walking by with feathers coming out of their butts and we find this the funniest thing on the planet. They know we're laughing at them but still smile with frozen million-dollar smiles. There's an Elvis impersonator outside on the street singing Sheryl Crow's "Leaving Las Vegas", and I croon along until the two of us are dancing like lovers. His sideburns tickle my cheek as he moves in for a kiss, but Evan says, "No way, Jose."

The lights are glitzy and we're sparkling along the Strip. We don't let go of one another. The Stardust and Sahara and Circus Circus Hotel and Casino. "Enter the Night", billed as the hottest show in town. We're high on life and each other. He's got a bottle and at first, he's hesitant to share it with me, not wanting me to slide back into any bad behavior, but I tell him that's ridiculous and that he doesn't have to worry about monitoring me. I'm WAY better than I was last spring, not as shattered by Kristen anymore, I think. At least at this moment. And look, we're still celebrating and we deserve to, so we spark a joint as well and the weed cools my lungs in the heat. We shotgun the smoke and fall into a make-out session. I want him so bad that I'll die if we're not together this night. I want to tell him I love him and birth his children so I can see his face in theirs. I want us to rob banks like a teenage Bonnie and Clyde and get shot outside some barn as our blood coalesces.

"This might just be the best night of my life," I say instead.

He nibbles on my lip. "Me too. Can you feel the electricity in the air?"

I don't know what he's talking about, but I nod that I do.

"Like, the Bouquets are on the cusp. It's crackling. You're gonna take us there."

My eyes grow wide. "Let's get a room," I say, tugging at him.

"What? We have—"

"No, I want only you tonight. No one else around."

We pool our money and find a motel just off the Strip. The neon sign flashes Vacancy but only the c-a-n are lit red. We pass over crumpled bills to a lady behind the desk in a housecoat with curlers in her hair. The room smells like dust and the bed creaks and the mattress feels like it's full of Slinkys poking into my back. The window doesn't face the Strip, only the vastness of the other side of Vegas, a seemingly endless desert that stretches out into oblivion. We leave off the lights and remove each other's clothes. His roomy sweater, my baby doll dress. He's lean with a tuft of blond hair on his chest in the shape of a cross. The butterflies in my stomach have gone into a tizzy and creep up my throat. We get under the covers and slip off the rest of our clothes. He's sweet and kind and gentle, unlike any of the other boys I've been with. He takes his time and asks if I'm okay because I'm tearing, but I tell him that I'm crying because I'm alive. He has protection in his jeans pocket and, like a ninja, leaps out of bed and places it on. He's pale in the blue moon light leaking inside. He's on top of me and I make sure not to close my eyes, to take it all in: the scar above his lip from when a cat scratched him as a kid, his nose that's a little crooked, eyes so blue he looks inhuman. Stars dance along the ceiling, a wave rushes through my body. I'm all goosebumps and delight. And when it's over I tell him to squeeze me tight enough to crush my bones. I've never been so secure.

At some point we fall asleep enmeshed, losing track of whose limbs are whose, until the sun bruises the morning by declaring its arrival.

***

"I'm gonna grab some chips," I say, my stomach rumbling. His face married to the pillow, no chance of waking yet. In the bathroom, my hair looks like I stuck it in a socket. I tame it down, wedge myself into my dress, and splash water on my face. My makeup has smeared and I appear crazy, but deliriously happy, like most crazy people are.

Outside I munch on Andy Capp's Hot Fries and cherry Mambas from the vending machine. I go to a pay phone booth and slip in some quarters and call my folks, telling them I'm okay and that the show went well. Then I ring Winter, and Jeremy answers.

"Nico Nicotine," he squeals. "Girl, I had a premonition that the call would be you. I've been very into my psychic abilities as of late."

"You're a regular Miss Cleo."

"She is my spirit animal. So how's the trip going?"

"Awesome, I mean, seriously amazing. Like the two shows were *phe*nom and then, okay, Evan and I finally slept together."

I hear him scream and have to pull the phone away from my ear.

"Nicola, all the deets."

"I mean, it wasn't like with any other guy. He was so, like, loving. I feel like I'm floating."

"He was soooo cute when I saw him," Jeremy says. "I would do things to that boy that would get his head to spin."

"I really like him."

"I'm happy for you. You deserve it. Like, Nico I'm living vicariously through you."

I squint my eyes from the barreling sun and shove a few more Hot Fries in my mouth. "So, Jer, how's the L.A. life?"

"Well, we went to this pool party at one of Emily's friends' house."

I stick my finger down my throat and mock-gag.

"Everyone was hella wasted, like we got home at four in the morning."

"Is Winter up?"

"No girl, she's dead, dead today. She was partying hard."

I feel a vice squeeze at my heart. "Oh yeah, what was she doing?"

"I mean, there were some drugs."

"Hard stuff?"

"I didn't partake! You know I'm not messing with anything that could screw up my skin. Coke makes ya blotchy."

"So, she was doing...?"

"I don't know. She went off with this guy. They call him Sasquatch. He's huge and hairy, he graduated a few years ago. She passed out when we got back, so I didn't really hear about it."

"Oh. Well, can you see if she's awake?"

"I'm poking her in the back right now and...nothing. I mean, I can see her breathing and all, but she ain't waking."

"Yeah, no, I understand."

"Maybe try later this afternoon?"

"We'll be driving to Denver for our next show."

"I'm sorry, Nico. She'll rip my head off if I keep poking. You know how she is."

"Yeah." I'm about to hang up, but something prevents me. "Can you...can you just look out for her, Jer, like make sure she's not doing any harder stuff. I mean, at least not too much."

"She's okay. She's like Keith Richards, she can handle anything. Her body's built that way."

"Okay...yeah, no I know."

"Don't worry about us. The next time you call, I'll make sure she gets on. She loves you, Nico."

Really? I think. *Because it doesn't seem much like that lately.*

"I love her too," I say, getting choked up. Whether he can hear it or not in my voice, he doesn't let on.

"Love ya, girl. Have a great tour. And buy me a lot of gifts on the road."

"I will…" But he's already hung up. Even though it's so hot, a chill whips through my bones. I'm shivering in my dress. The power of Winter to scare. I'm scared for her. I don't want to admit it and ruin my tour but I am. I hang up the phone and a flood of vomit pours out of me like an erupting volcano, the Hot Fries not even digested, melting on the pavement like curled orange blobs. Here I'd been worrying about Winter, but how much alcohol and pot had I consumed?

I leave my sick frying on the pavement. It's time to motor out of Las Vegas. It's not healthy to stay here any longer than we already have. I know that I'm susceptible to temptation, something I'll have to watch out for if I ever really become a rockstar. Like my former hero Cobain, I've seen how too easily it can fester and destroy.

6

• • • • •

River of Deceit – Mad Season

We play a stellar show at Ax Grinder in Denver, the venue set-up to look like a log cabin. The band forming a synchronicity. I'm no longer on the outside looking in, establishing myself to be a full-ranking member too. I still only sing "Violet" and "The Sign" at the end, but once again, that's where the crowd truly gets amped. After the show, we find out we got a hella dope write-up in Guitar Picks. A half page is devoted to a pic of us holding guitar picks with me pretending to slit my throat. Someone flipping through the mag would assume I'm the lead singer and not Clarissa. The journalist especially focuses on my stage presence during "Violet" and how I kept them all rapt during "The Sign". We decide to camp in the mountains as a jubilee before our next leg.

We go to the Garden of the Gods about two hours from the city where the grasslands meet the pinon-jumper woodlands with Pike's Peak as the backdrop. The air so fresh and pure it makes me wonder why I've wasted so much time in my life in a smog-pit like L.A. Orange-brown rock cliffs against a pool-blue sky and a dash of trees scattered throughout like Bob Ross or someone painted it. It's fully dark by the time we reach a spot and set-up tents. I can hear animal sounds since there's no one else but us around. In a pot over a fire, I cook franks and beans and think of my favorite scene in *Blazing Saddles* where all the cowboys are farting.

Ed rolls a fat spliff. We talk about the article and give kudos to Lacey for making it happen. We heat up some whiskey and pass that around in old mugs because it's cold. The stars are out and winking and Kristen's on my mind, but I don't want her there because I'm having a good time and don't want to get sad. So I push her away, whether she likes it or not.

I'm half-sitting in Evan's lap and he's combing my hair with his lean fingers. Ed and Randy are going shot for shot with one another, and Randy takes out a boombox and puts in my mixtape. "River of Deceit" by Mad Season comes on and we all stand and sway under the moon. The blunt gets passed my way. For a second, I'm hesitant since we smoked yesterday, and Evan even looks at me like I don't have to toke, especially after I got a little out of control after Cobain died. But things were so different then. I was still reeling from Kristen's death and mad at Cobain. I know I have to monitor my pot and alcohol intake, but I did deserve to celebrate more after some great shows, right? So I let myself take only one big hit and cough and cough until it feels like my lungs are being torn apart.

"I love you guys so much," Randy says, and we all yell how much we love him too. Clarissa's quiet, focusing on ripping one cigarette after another. We get in a group hug around the small fire, our faces lit and sparkling, the music reaching a crescendo. I see Randy pulling Evan closer, his hand rubbing Evan's chest. The group hug breaks up, but Randy keeps grabbing Evan. All of a sudden, Randy's tongue is in Evan's ear. Evan jerks away.

"What, man?" Randy says. He's smiling but looks like he wants to cry.

Evan shakes his head. "No, no."

"C'mon," Randy says, pulling him close again. He goes to kiss his neck.

"No," Evan says, louder this time and pushing him, hard enough for Randy to fall over. Ed goes to help him up, but Randy swats his hand away.

"I love him," I hear Randy say, like a mewling cat, and then he's crying. It's hard to watch a grown man cry. It makes me feel icky and uncomfortable.

Evan reaches out his hand to help Randy up. "I love you too, man. But not like that. I'm sorry."

Randy still sits there in the dirt. We hear a howl in the distance and my spine chills.

"C'mon, man," Evan says, "Let's get you to bed."

Ed helps Randy to his feet. He lops Randy's arm around his neck. "I'm sorry, I'm sorry," Randy says. "I'm so stupid."

"No, you're not, man," Evan says. "You're amazing. We're all amazing."

"I love you guys," Randy says, before Ed takes him away.

Evan shrugs at me. "I've told him before that I'm not interested. He does this from time to time."

Clarissa makes a sound under her breath that echoes in the mountains. It sounds like she says, "you toy with everyone".

"I try to be nice about it with him," Evan says, his eye on Clarissa. "I don't want to hurt anyone's feelings."

I wrap my arms around his waist, as Clarissa hops up like she's gotten a burst of energy. She's got a bottle in hand and pours alcohol into mugs she brings over to me and Evan.

"We need to still cheers," she says. In the dark only lit by the fire, she's just red lips speaking. "We can't let this ruin the party."

"Cheers!" Lacey giggles, sitting by the fire and raising her own mug before gulping it down.

I take the mug and smell what seems like gasoline. "What is it?"

"My signature cocktail," she says, clinking her own mug with mine. "Bound to put hair on your tongue."

Evan and I look at each other and laugh. We take a sip, and it tastes terrible, but I figure one last drink won't kill me.

"I mean, the Bouquets are in a magazine," she says, dipping her head back to the night sky. "Like, this is the start of something big."

"Woo hoo," Evan says, taking another chug.

"And the bulk of the article was about you, Nico," she says, as I can see yellow in her pupils. Like an animal, she prowls around the fire. "Isn't that just the funniest thing?"

Evan's laughing but I'm not. I see where she's going with this. I take another sip and then regret it.

"Like you're *in* the Bouquets, Nico. Like it's a

foregone conclusion."

"She *is* in the Bouquets," Evan says. "Why can't we have two singers, you and her?"

I continue taking more sips. Now they're arguing but it's hard to follow what they're saying. In fact, everything starts to go hazy. The sky like tar drips and drips and the stars are so bright they hurt my eyes. My stomach expands until it feels like I'm pregnant. I run into a thicket of trees and let my insides out. It's all over my hands and I'm freaking out because it seems like my vomit is coming to life, swarming over my body until I'm trapped in a cocoon of sickness. I can't break free. The surrounding animals become louder, more insidious, vicious teeth snapping, claws scraping. I scream but it's so far down within myself that it's barely a peep. I want to cry but have no tears left. I run, my feet out of control, tripping over myself, until I'm thrust back into the campfire. I look for Lacey who was sitting on a log earlier, but she's gone. And then, right by the fire, Evan's shirt gets ripped open as Clarissa prowls above him, licking his nipple and then moving in for a kiss. She's watching me the whole time with a devilish grin. I scream loud enough to scare myself and run back into the woods, the image of their deceit playing over and over again. Now the fire is so far away that it's only darkness. I'm alone. I'm cold, only wearing a flannel. I'll never forgive Evan. He lied to me when he said he didn't have feelings for Clarissa anymore. The two of them will always have a connection, and it didn't matter if they were inebriated. Alcohol brings out your true emotions.

"Kristen, where are you?" I hear myself saying,

needing her to soothe. I tuck myself into a fetal position, the dirt my pillow. I'm crying into my mouth. A hand touches my cheek that's light as a feather, the notion of a hand rather than an actual one. It doesn't belong to Evan, even though if it was, I would've rejected it at the moment. It belongs to someone who's transcended and left space and time, my dead sister reborn as something different.

"Sssssssh," she tells me. She no longer speaks because she's no longer connected to her human form. Telepathically she warns me to go near the fire or I'll freeze. She picks up my weary limbs and brings me there, the fire beckoning. No one surrounds it anymore, everyone retreated into their tents. I fall asleep with the flames kissing my face, my chills subsided, my anger still red hot. A vision of Evan and Clarissa burning behind my eyes, infiltrating my dreams.

7

• • • • •

Hurt – Nine Inch Nails

Ed and Randy find me in the morning shivering. The fire has gone out, the morning chilly even though it's summer. I sit up in a daze, reconstructing memories from last night. Us hugging around the fire, Randy telling Evan he loves him, and then the poison I drank, a cocktail of evil that Clarissa conjured and had to be spiked with something. Running off into the woods and then finding Evan with his shirt open and Clarissa licking his nipple. Ed and Randy make jokes about me being too wasted to find my tent, but I tell them to shut up.

"Where is Evan?" I ask, and they shrug. He didn't make it back to the guys' tent last night. I look over at Clarissa's and see Evan emerge in long john bottoms and no shirt. One of his eyes is shut closed with crust and one side of his hair has been mashed into the shape of a ramp. He scratches at his stubble and gives a confused wave.

"Oh, hell no," I declare, throwing my arms up at

the sky and booking it away from all of them. I'm stewing as I run down to a river that snakes through our campsite. Everything is blurry because I'm crying. I splash water on my face until I can't distinguish my tears any longer. The evidence is there that Evan slept with Clarissa last night, and it doesn't even matter if Clarissa slipped something in our drinks. Like I didn't find my way into Ed and Randy's tent and do them. I remember Clarissa saying under her breath that Evan "toys with everyone" and our whole relationship becomes slanted. Had he told me what I wanted to hear rather than what he truly felt? I couldn't forget that he was a freshman in college while I'm still in high school. He may have bedded hundreds of girls and I was nothing more than a conquest. I spit out the lake water like I'm spitting in his face and make my way back to the campsite.

Everyone is packing up, and Ed says that "we should leave in ten since it's a long drive to our next stop in Chicago."

Evan comes over to me, but I don't even want to look at him.

"Hey," he says.

"Hey yourself."

"Wha…?" I hear him say as I motor it to the van. I get in and sit in the back, arms crossed. I can't imagine traveling for the next fourteen hours with a Judas like him. I hope Clarissa gave him a bug that makes his dick fall off.

I lean against the window and pretend I'm sleeping while everyone gets inside. Out of the corner of my eye, I can see that Evan is wise enough to sit in the seat in front of me, although Clarissa is next to him. I feel Lacey put her palm on my shoulder.

"Are you okay, Nico?" she asks, and I'm certainly not mad at her but don't want to talk to anyone.

"No," I say, as a tear spills salty into my lips.

"What happened last night?" Lacey asks, as Ed revs up the van and we drive out of the campsite. My mixtape is still in the cassette player and "Hurt" from Nine Inch Nails comes on, mirroring what more than half of us in the van are feeling.

When I see Clarissa whispering something into Evan's ear, my eye snaps open like a pulled shade and I nearly lunge at the wench.

"What did you just say to him?" I yell at her. Up front, Ed and Randy are like, *la, la, la, I'm not a part of this.*

"Uh, take a chill pill," Clarissa says. "I asked if he wanted some gum."

She holds up a pack of Chewles and it reminds me of a time when Evan and I kissed and the goo from his gum squirted into my mouth. I go ballistic.

"What did you put in our drinks?"

Clarissa places her hand over her heart in mock-shock. "What are you talking about, Nico?"

"You roofied us!"

Clarissa bursts out laughing and looks around the van for support. "You just can't handle your liquor."

I go to leap over the seat, but Lacey holds me back.

"Nico, calm down," Lacey says.

"No, she's been trying to put a wedge between me and Evan since I got here. She's hella shady."

I look over at Evan and he's gotten all small, tucked

into the corner like he doesn't want to be noticed.

"I saw her on top of you, Evan," I'm saying. Snot and tears muffle my accusations but the intent is obvious. "You had your shirt off and she was licking your nipple." I point to the succubus.

"I don't remember much," Evan says, with a shrug, as if that's all he has to defend himself.

"Look, Nico," Clarissa says, in this mom voice. "You had a lot of pot and alcohol and not everyone is capable of mixing the two. I don't want Evan. I cheated on Evan a long time ago, and like, we're done."

Evan's chewing on the end of his lip.

"You threatened me in the bathroom at Elvis' Last Toilet."

She rolls her eyes. "No, Nico, I just said that relationships can destroy a band. I was giving you girl-to-girl advice. Like, you're young, you're so young. We're in college and you're in high school and you just haven't had all the experiences that we have."

"But I'm a better singer than you."

Clarissa lets out a sharp cackle. "I don't know about that."

"Everyone in the Bouquets has said so. And the article in Guitar Picks focused on me. He didn't even mention you."

"You're a child."

"And you're Lucifer."

She palms her forehead. "I don't even know what that means. Guys, she's unhinged."

No one else in the van speaks, the Nine Inch Nails song piercing through the tension in the air.

I cross my arms again in a huff. "I may be unhinged

but you're obsolete."

Evan finally trains his blue eyes on me. "I really don't remember last night," he says, softly as if he doesn't want Clarissa to overhear.

"I don't care. It doesn't take away what you did. Can you admit that you still have feelings for her, so we can all just move on?"

"I don't think you wanna hear his answer, honey," Clarissa says. She has her compact out and is putting on mascara.

"You shut it, or I'll shut it for you," I say, raising my fist.

"I mean, is this what you all want to deal with?" Clarissa asks, looking around the van. "Everything sets her off. We didn't have problems like this before she came along."

Ed pipes up. "Can we just listen to the music with you *all* shutting up? I have to drive for fourteen god-damn hours and will take this van off of the road."

"Fine by me," Clarissa says, and puts headphones over her ears cranking up her own beats.

"I'm sorry," Evan mouths to me. "I really don't remember what happened." He seems honest, but I don't care right now. It's not even six in the morning and I'm tired and want to sleep. I have a show tonight I need to get ready for.

And I also have to figure out how I can mess with Clarissa on stage. This she-beast won't get off the hook with what she did.

Nico's revenge is coming.

8

• • • • • •

Seether – Veruca Salt

When we get to the venue in Chicago, Lacey pulls us into a powwow because a chainsaw couldn't cut the thick tension between all of us. I'm mad at Evan, Clarissa hates me, Evan doesn't know what to think about Clarissa or me at this point, Randy still has a torch for Evan, and Ed's fisting two beers—now I know what Fleetwood Mac must've gone through on the reg. Anyway, Lacey gives us a pep talk like we're all this together while Clarissa and I slice each other apart with our eyes. Luckily, I slept a lot on the ride over, plotting sweet revenge in my dreams.

"We've got this momentum," Lacey says, a true cheerleader. "We have an amazing write-up in a magazine. That could lead to people in the business being at the show. You never know."

Ed puts down his beers. "Hell, I'm ready. I'm not getting caught-up in teenage bullshit."

"You know I'm not," Randy says, because he's thirty. Even though he's the most teenage of us all.

"Like, it's cool," I say, completely acting unaffected even though I'm seething with rage. "Yesterday's news. I'm ready to fuckin' sing."

I give myself devil horns and stick out my tongue.

"That's what I want to hear," Lacey says. "Clarissa?"

Clarissa's ripping into her cigarette, a scowl taking over her face. "Like, I'm cool too. I'm cooler than Antarctica. Brrrr. And now I need to powder my nose."

She trails off, good riddance to the skank.

"Nico, can we…?" Evan starts to ask, hands shoved in pockets, whistling out of the side of his mouth.

Ed, Randy, and Lacey take this as a cue and scuttle away. Now that we're left alone, I'm too exhausted to stay angry at him. He so looks like a sad puppy. But I can't have him think he can get away with treating me this way.

"Evan, you… I'm upset because you didn't stand up for me."

I try not to get over-emotional but it's not easy.

"I didn't…" He kicks at an empty beer can. "I didn't understand what happened."

"She drugged us," I say. "It was super sketchy. End of story."

"I can't imagine Clarissa would do something like that."

"Ugh. You're blinded because you used to *do* her. She's Shady McShade. And are you sorry for how you treated me, or do you want me to, like, give her a pass?"

"I'm sorry!" He goes to hug me but I'm not ready yet. I can tell this destroys him, and I enjoy that kind of power. "I think it's cause, well, I never liked someone as much as I like you. I don't know how to deal with that," he says.

He's legit almost crying and I know not feeding me some b.s. We're on stage in like ten minutes so I let him hug me, and honestly, it feels so good.

"I brought you into this band, and I just wanted everything to be perfect," he says. "Between you and I, between you and the band."

He's resting his chin on the top of my head because he's that much taller. I imagine his tears dropping into my hair.

"It's not gonna be perfect," I say, surprised by this wise surge in me. "No band is. That's why they all break up so much, or end in…"

We both know where I'm going with this—Kurt Cobain. Like Kristen, at times, he has the ability to resurface and spear my heart.

Evan ends the hug. "So, truce?" His baby blues begging me for relief. I hold on a second longer to make him sweat.

"Yeah," I say, punching him hard in the shoulder. "Truce."

"Ow, Nico," he says, but he's laughing.

"That's a warning. Don't fuck with Nico."

He throws his hands up in the air. "I never plan on it again."

***

During the band's first few songs, I've got my Sports Walkman on with the mixtape I'd left in the van's cassette player. Instead of listening to "Violet", which

I'm about to tear the crap out of on stage, I'm playing Veruca Salt's "Seether" over and over to amp me up. I'm a fireball of pure and beautiful rage with Clarissa as my bullseye. She doesn't even know what she's in for.

I fix my boobs in my baby doll dress, the same one I wore at the last show, now musty with a line of dirt on the edges of the tulle. I hear my name being called by Evan and hand over my Walkman to Lacey as I jump up on stage, my Doc Martins landing with a thud.

"Hello, Chicago, your pizza sucks," I say, and spit a piece of pink bubblegum at the crowd. It's even bigger than our last show, and I wonder if the write-up in Guitar Picks has anything to do with it. "We are Grenade Bouquets and this is our deliciously horrific cover of Hole's "Violet"."

The first guitar licks ramp up as I whisper, "And the sky was made of amethysts." I build to the chorus and scream into the mic like a vampire out for blood. The crowd erupts into a mosh pit. Clarissa tries to muscle in on the song, but she's no match for a tiger like me. I growl as she backs off, my voice sung to the back of the room and out into Chicago's streets. Clarissa's a baby fawn, barely a yelp, meaningless. I'm singing it directly at her now, my pupils spinning and wild, a spray of spit in her face, as the guitars go nuts. I'm straddling the mic stand now, its cord wrapped around me like a snake, my mouth so wide the crowd can see my back molars.

"One above and one below," I sing, like a demon is birthing from my canal. Clarissa is close, struggling to keep up, and I leave her in my goddamn dust. "I get what I want, but I never want it again."

She turns toward me as I pull my fist back and clock her right in her smug little pinched face. I feel cheekbone as I connect, and she loses balance, tumbling into the audience like a ballerina on crack. Since they don't expect her downfall, no one catches her and she lands like a giant bag of dirt on the floor as the fans see God and I keep them in my spell through the final lyrics. "Go on take everything," I sing, stamping around, peering over at Clarissa who tries to rise to her feet with the shakiest knees on the planet. The crowd pushes her around, dislodging brilliant tears from her eye sockets, as I bring the song to a delirious finish. My knuckles are bruised and I wipe the blood emerging across my face with sly smile.

I glance at the rest of the Bouquets who slowly stop playing in shock, but the crowd is eating it up with a huge fuckin' ice cream spoon.

"Nico triumphant," I tell them, making a muscle as they chant my name back. I bathe in their adoration and the chanting of my name, knowing I have them locked once I'll wrap this shit up with "The Sign".

Ed, Randy, and Evan shrug at one another while playing the opening chords, and with that, Clarissa has been made irrelevant.

Sorry, not sorry, trick.

9

• • • • •

Unglued – Stone Temple Pilots

"Hey, Winter," I say, into the motel's phone. The rest of the band is at the bar downstairs drinking cocktails, but I'm thinking about Winter because we didn't leave things copacetic between us. She's been my best friend since we were eleven, and I need to tell someone about slugging Clarissa at the show. Speaking of Clarissa, no one's seen her since she fled from the stage after I knocked her out cold. To avoid any type of fallout from it, I scurried upstairs while the band sank into their drinks. So maybe I'm calling Winter because I'm worried about her, or maybe she's just an excuse so I can avoid any fallout.

"Heyyyyyy," she says, after a moment of silence that stretches for eons. It sounds like she's smoking, and not cigarettes, since she takes large inhales between each suck.

"Did I wake you?" I ask. I look at my Swatch watch that I got for my thirteenth birthday and it's after midnight.

"I don't sleep," she says. "I'm a vampire." The way she says it is not sarcastic like the old Winter, but sad and lonely like sleep is her worst enemy.

"I just finished a show. I'm in Chicago."

Our convos have never been stilted like this. We used to be able to talk about anything for hours, the conversation bending and weaving into unchartered territories so easily. Now it seems like I'm bothering her.

"Chicago," she says, as if she's pissed with it. "Like what is the Midwest even? What's the point? America should just be the coasts and that's it. Oh, shit."

"What?"

"My cigarette...like it's burning."

"So put it out."

"Really, Nico, is that what you do with a cigarette? Thanks for the enlightening tip."

"I can call back another time—"

"No, no, I'm alive now. So...?"

I try to make my voice more chipper. "So, yeah, we played this show in Chicago, and at our last one got a write-up in a magazine."

I hear her take the longest drag of her cigarette.

"That pot?" I ask.

She gulps. "It's not pot."

My stomach churns, my mind racing at what else she could be smoking? It's late and, like, a Wednesday night, and she seems as if she's firmly exiting reality.

"Niiiiicccoooooo, Niiiiiccccoooooo," she says, as if it's a little song. "Nico, my Nico. So, you sang?"

"I gotta tell you about Evan's ex—".

"Who's Evan?"

I pinch the bridge of my nose. "My boyfriend..."

It feels weird saying it out loud, but that's what Evan is—my boyfriend at the bar downstairs sipping on a gimlet.

"Right, right, the Cobain-looking motherfucker," Winter says. I picture her looking at all her new Marilyn Manson posters and thinking to herself that she's so much cooler than when she used to obsess over Vedder and all the other grunge leading men.

"Yeah, so his ex is in the band too and she's been giving me hell, so when we were on stage, I punched her right in the face and sent her into the mosh pit. The crowd went wild."

I perk up from remembering how my fist felt against her face. Winter doesn't even bother to respond. I'm barely worth her time.

"Ya-know, I think about how we used to worship these singers," she says. "You and Cobain, me and Vedder, Jeremy and Chris Cornell, and we thought the music had so much meaning, but they're really all sell-outs. Like, how much has each of them made off of their success? No longer about the music anymore."

"Is Marilyn Manson any different?"

She laughs in a superior way. I imagine she's shaking her head.

"Manson is like anti-establishment. He doesn't want to fit into the norm. He's not grunge. He's his own creation." I hear a rustling sound. "No, Emily, just like, light it."

"Oh," I say, as my stomach turns. "Emily's there?"

Winter giggles like a witch. "Yeah, Emily's always kinda here. I mean, like she didn't *move* in, move in, but kinda."

"She doesn't have a home of her own?"

"She has a home, but if you must know, she's having parental problems, so…"

"No, I get it, I get it."

"Do you?"

"Yes, I do, Winter. I mean, I had a lot of problems with my parents too."

"It's not the same. Like, your parents didn't talk about their feelings enough or whatever, Emily's dealing with some major heavy stuff. So, I'm like here for her."

"O…kay."

"Is it okay, Nico? Do I have your permission?"

I clutch the phone like I'm trying to break it. "Do you have a problem with me, Winter? You seem like you want to start something."

"Hey, I'm not starting anything."

"I call to check up on you and—"

"Check up on me?" The vibrato in her voice becomes vicious. I can tell when Winter's out for blood and she's become unglued. I just had never been the target of her rage until recently. "Oh, Nico's so perfect since she had her little runaway adventure and found a boyfriend and sings in a band. Shall I bow down?"

The room gets very hot all of a sudden like someone's beneath the floors cooking me.

"I'm not asking—"

"Insufferable," I hear, and I don't know if it's Emily or Winter who said it, but it doesn't really matter because the way they're laughing tells me they've formed an unbreakable unit and I'm on the outside.

I don't know how to respond. I'm angry and not crying yet but I know I will. Their cackles grow in power, insidiously traveling through the phone cord into my soul. I quietly hang up as if it means that the conversation never happened. But I'm not that good a pretender.

The door opens and Evan walks inside while I'm in full sob.

"Hey, hey," he says, wrapping his long arms around me. "Don't worry about what happened with Clarissa."

I pull some Kleenex from the tissue box and dab my eyes. "That's not why I'm crying."

"Because I have to admit it turned me on." He starts kissing my ear and his breath smells like gin.

"It's my friend Winter. I don't think we're gonna be friends much longer."

"I'm sorry."

"Yeah, me too."

"She seemed... I dunno."

"No, you can say it."

"Difficult, and she didn't like me."

"Don't take offense, she hates most people."

"Look, she's far away in L.A. Don't worry about her. You'll fix whatever you need to fix when you get home."

"Yeah, you're right."

"And if not, you'll just pop her in the face like you did to Clarissa."

I hit his shoulder in a friendly way. He tickles my ribs and then we're making out and Winter isn't a thought anymore. I push her all the way into the recesses of my mind until she transforms into a tiny nuisance, no bigger than a gnat that I can squash if need be.

Besides, it's the heart of the summer, and I ain't got time for any Winter shit.

10

· · · · ·

Bad Reputation – Freedy Johnston

I gotta give credit to Clarissa, since she stayed out of my hair on the drive to our next show in Philadelphia. Now we're at the venue The Note and she's all the way on the other side of the bar sucking down her drink. Every so often, I look her way and cut her with my eyes, but she doesn't respond. She's probably ruminating about her place in the band and how much I've wedged my way in. *And* how no one took her side after the punch. The Bouquets are made up of boys who've punched each other before to get over any squabbles and figure it's sexist to think that girls should be any different.

Lacey is next to me doing number crunching about how much we've spent at motels plus gas versus what we've made so far.

"I think we're up fifty bucks," she says, and I can't tell if that means it's a success or not. "No, that's good," she continues, and rubs my shoulder. "We've *never* been up before, so it's a start. This venue's getting packed too."

I glance around and this might just be our biggest crowd yet. There's a solid group of people in front of the stage. Since we're the first band on, it can't all be for the headliner.

"Excuse me," I hear, and turn around on my stool to a girl around my age with a lip ring, an eyebrow ring, and dyed hair the color of a Sunkist. "Are you in that Grenade band?"

"Yeah, the Grenade Bouquets," I say, acting like it's no big deal for a fan to come up to me. "Why?"

"Hey, Phoebe," the girl yells, and an equally-pierced girl shows up with smudged makeup and lemon-dyed hair. "We've heard about you punching the other girl in your band."

"So bad-ass," Phoebe says, chewing on her lip ring.

"Yeah, I did." I eye Lacey. "And I'll do it again if she crosses me."

I nod over to Clarissa, who still hasn't looked up from her drink, but I give her the finger anyway. The two girls are awestruck.

"Whoa," the first one says. "You guys really hate each other."

"She's trying to get in between me and my man."

I point over to Evan, who's drinking a pint in the corner with Ed and Randy. Evan flips his long hair out of his eyes and gives a wave.

"She deserves it," Phoebe says. "C'mon, let's make sure we get a front row spot in case there's any blood."

I give her devil horns in response, and the girls make their way toward the stage.

"You got a bad reputation, Nico," Lacey says, wagging her pen at me.

"And it isn't just talk, talk, talk," I say, quoting the Freedy Johnston song.

"Look, it's filling up even more. Maybe everyone's heard about your tussle?"

A stream of Gen Xers rush through the opening door. There's enough of a crowd so it really feels like a show with a legit band. But then I realize I *am* a part of a legit band.

"No publicity's bad publicity," Lacey says. "The two most famous people all year were Nancy Kerrigan and Tonya Harding."

Who could forget when Tonya Harding clubbed Nancy Kerrigan at the Winter Olympics and Nancy Kerrigan cried, "Whyyyy me?"

"Which one am I?" I ask, with a wicked grin knowing I was veering into Tonya Harding territory.

"Which one do you want to be?"

I mime like I'm clubbing Lacey's leg.

"Remind me to never get on your wrong side, Nico," she says.

Evan, Ed, and Randy come over. "So, we've had like three folks come up to us about the punch," Ed says. "One said he came to this show because it seems like our band is like a grenade about to go off. I think he said it because of our name too."

"Yeah, those two girls talking to us heard about it," I say.

"Nico the knockout," Randy says, and raises my hand to the ceiling like I'd won a fight in a ring.

Evan kisses me on the cheek. "My girl's a little fighter."

I see Clarissa glance over and then knock back the

rest of her drink, crunching hard on the ice.

"She won't get over this easily," Evan says, massaging his forehead. "The two of us would fight like hell, and she'd never let it end. She's figuring out how to get back at you."

"Let her," I say. "I'm not afraid." I crack my knuckles. "We'll give 'em a show."

***

When the set starts, I can see Clarissa is subdued and not acting like herself. She's lifeless during the Lemonheads duet with Evan. The band introduces me and I storm up on stage, staring her down like we're wrestlers entering an arena. The cool licks of Hole's "Violet" begin, and I thrash around the stage, a tornado demolishing everything in its path. Clarissa is trying to keep up, but her voice gets drowned out. As the song quiets down, I stand in place singing, "Get what I want but I never want it again." The music ramps up and Clarissa takes a swing at me but misses entirely. She swings hard enough to almost fall over. I have a beer bottle in hand and swig from it before spitting out the suds in her face. The crowd erupts, the mosh pit reaching a crescendo. Clarissa has beer in her fried hair and her makeup is stained. She comes at me with her talons out. We wrestle around but I have about twenty pounds on this dumb Tweedy Bird and she doesn't stand a chance. She's growling, she's cursing, she's digging in her nails, but I flip her over and the crowd goes, "Whoa" and she falls hard on her tailbone. I pick up the song right where I'd been so rudely interrupted and bring it to its beautiful conclusion. She's stewing on the stage as the lights dim once the song ends. When they brighten, she's already gone. I stick my tongue out at the crowd wide enough to show off my uvula. I give them a tubular shaka sign before swallowing some more beer and spitting it into the air too.

"We're Grenade Bouquets," I yell. "And you won't fucking forget us!"

I make a fist to show I mean business and they get even crazier, screaming for more.

There's a rush through my body like my blood is made up of glitter and I'm hooked. I never want to come down. I'm throbbing—a quasar of pure energy. Shining bright, blinding on the stage.

Primed to explode.

11

• • • • •

Chelsea Morning – Joni Mitchell

I wake up in New York City for the first time ever in a motel in the neighborhood Chelsea and Evan's playing his guitar and singing "Chelsea Morning" by Joni Mitchell. I know of the song because it's one of my Aunt Carly's favorite records. We drove through the night in the van from Philly after the show, all of us loud and pumped except for Clarissa who remained mute. We had reputations now, the indie band who wasn't afraid to fight with one another. There's a buzz building around our final show in New York. We're the opening, opening band at the Rusted Nail, and I can feel the energy crackling in the air, lightning in our veins. We all got separate motel rooms and Evan and I made love last night while sipping from a Scotch bottle. Now he's singing Joni Mitchell to me and I have a moony smile on my face as if I want everything to stay like this forever. After a year of being sad because of Kristen, I no longer feel like a muddy puddle. She hovers on the periphery but is no longer set to knife my heart.

"What do you want to do today before the show?" Evan asks, putting down the guitar. He's shirtless, wearing boxers and knee-high socks like an eighties' jock, although I know he's wearing them ironically. His hair is mussed and he has a fine layer of blond stubble for a beard. I reach over and put on a Reading Rainbow tee I've had since I was a kid and is perfectly shrunken and yellowed now.

"I want to see New York," I say, getting up and looking out of the window. We face a back alley and a rat crawls along the windowsill. I turn to him. "A better view of New York."

So, we have a breakfast of grilled cheese sandwiches at Eisenberg Diner. I love how the place has a 50's vibe with stools in front of a long bar and a waitress taking our orders with a cigarette dangling from her lips. She takes a suck and leaves a kiss of red on the cigarette's tip. Her accent is full Noo Yawk asking us if we want "cawfee". We munch on our grilled cheeses, and Evan tells me something that makes the hairs on my arm stand tall.

"You really have it," he says.

"What?" I signal the waitress for a coffee refill.

"Star quality. Like, you own the stage, Nico."

The waitress pours more cawfee and I take a hot sip.

"You're gonna take us into uncharted territory," Evan says. "I can feel it—"

I nod because I feel it as well. A breeze of the diner's AC seems to whisper my name. My stomach is all twisty and turny, the near future shimmering, the potential for us all to soar. He scoops up my hand and kisses a knuckle.

We head to the Met and wander around. My favorite part being the knights, those massive armored statues posed as if guarding the museum. Wide-eyed kids on camp tours point, and I have a flash of wondering what it could be like to be famous. People pointing at me. Could I wander around like this, or will I have to wear sunglasses and a baseball cap? Evan and I are holding hands, and I wonder if he'll be part of my future? Will we survive what we'll become? Then I spiral back to Earth since so far, we're just a band who's played a few shows and got some attention because I fought on stage.

Outside we get Toasted Almond ice cream pops from a vendor, and walk through Central Park. It's hot and sunny and the city is alive. Sunbathers on a hill, children laughing and playing ball, games of football, nannies with strollers, and a man looking through a telescope at a hawk perched in a tree. We lie down and take a nap in the sun, his chest my pillow. When we wake, it's later and the sun has moved behind a cloud and the grass is colder.

"I wrote a song," I tell him. It'd been the one about my sister called "Ready to Guide" that I sang at her tombstone. It dealt with me not needing to be haunted by her ghost anymore.

"Do you want to sing it at the show tonight?"

I sit up, paw my blue hair, and chew on the side of my lip.

"Really? I mean, the band hasn't even practiced..."

"Sing it for me now."

He's smiling so wide. I glance around like I'm nervous that someone could be watching.

"Nico, who cares who sees you here? You're gonna have a lot more eyes on you tonight."

I clear my throat and begin: "Your ghost remains inside, ready to guide..." I give the song the same beat as I did for the cover of Ace of Base's "The Sign". Evan drums against his chest. Singing about Kristen forces me to replay the day she died, that awful fucking Halloween when she dropped dead of a brain aneurism on a run. There are moments when my sadness affects the song, makes the lyrics go all shaky, but I power through. There's a hint of a tear in the corner of my eye, but that's all. An older couple nearby stop and clap.

"You have a beautiful voice, child," the old woman says.

I wipe away the tear and nod, "thank you".

"I think we have our next hit," Evan says.

We decide to walk back to our motel in Chelsea, past the Plaza Hotel and down 5th Avenue until we reach Madison Square Park and have to step over the crack vials on the ground. Homeless people huddle on benches because it's started to drizzle. One begs for money, and I search in my pocket and pull out two quarters.

"That all you got?" he asks, and so Evan gives him a dollar more.

"Couple of kids, couple of kids," he says, through the three teeth left in his mouth. He shakes his head. I have no idea what he means.

We get slices of pizza because Evan tells me that's what you have to do in New York no matter what. The cheese is hot and sticks to the roof of my mouth but it's delicious. Our bellies are full. We go see the movie *The Crow* and when we make it back to the motel, take a shower together. I'm washing his back and trace my finger around his tattoo of an American flag with an X through it.

"Down with America?" I ask.

"Yeah, I got it when my brother came home messed up from Iraq. Sometimes I regret it."

It stands out against his pale skin, and I can't help but think how it will look when the two of us are old. I've been picturing us this way more and more lately, linked as a unit until death. It both scares and excites me.

After the shower, he's got a towel around his waist and lights a cigarette as he plays the notes to my song, "Ready to Guide". When I sing along, it sounds right, like the two of us have created magic. The drizzle turns into a downpour plinking against the windowsill like cymbals, and our whole world is right there in this motel room, playing my song over and over till the end of time.

When we finish, he goes into the bathroom to shave and I make a Collect call to my mom first.

"Of course, I'll accept the charges," she says. "Nico?"

"Yeah, hi, Mom."

"Sweetie, you sound—well, you sound good."

"I am." I twist the phone cord around my finger. "It's been amazing. I can't believe this is our last show. New York City has been…"

Mom launches into this story how she went to New York once in high school on a trip and they saw the Statue of Liberty. I let her talk and don't interrupt. The old, surly Nico would've rolled her eyes.

"Lady Liberty was so much bigger than I expected. And we went up into the crown!"

"That's really cool, Mom."

"Oh, enough about that. So, the shows have gone well?"

"Yeah," I say, gushing. "We got a write-up in a magazine."

"A magazine?"

"Yeah, Mom, and like the focus was on me."

"She got a write-up in a magazine," I hear her tell Mr. Ferguson, and he says something muffled in response. "Oh, Nico, I'm so proud. And you're eating okay?"

"Yeah, I just had a slice of pizza. Um, I'm gonna sing this song tonight…it's about Kristen."

"Oh," Mom replies, and I can tell she's thinking about what to say next.

"I wrote it for her—well, about her too. It's about moving on, I mean, keeping her memory but moving on."

"Of course." She takes a deep breath. "Of course, honey."

"I love you, Mom," I say, my voice getting scratchy.

"I love you too, honey."

"I'll see you soon," I say, and hang up the phone. I make a Collect call to my dad next.

"Hey, Scrap," he says. "Lemme turn down the news. In Hawaii, this elephant just crushed his trainer to death."

"Ouch."

"So, how's the tour?"

"Good, I just talked to Mom. I told her I'm singing

this song for our last show tonight. It's about Kristen."

Unlike Mom, Dad never shows emotions, but I can hear him breathing heavier. We'd all been going to therapy over the summer, encouraged to talk more about Kristen, that it's okay to say her name.

"I'm glad it's going so well," he says, and then reca-librates. "And I'm sure…I'm sure your sister would've been your number one fan."

"Yeah, she'd…um…she'd definitely be proud to see how far I've come."

"We all are, Nico. Now are you being safe? No alcohol or drugs?"

"Yes, Dad."

"Remember, someone hands you a drink, you decline."

"I know, I know."

"You take care now. Love you."

"I love you too, Dad."

When I hang up, there's a quick image of Kristen outside of the window in the rain. She's not as formed as she used to be, more ghostly and heaven-like. She gives me a nod with her kind eyes, happy to see how much the relationship between me and the 'rents have changed. How hard we've all worked. How we've tried to understand each other better, even though we're not a complete family anymore. How we did it for her.

I'm singing "Ready to Guide" as Evan comes out of the bathroom in a shirt with holes in it and torn jeans, his face smooth from a fresh shave.

"You ready to stun 'em tonight?" he asks and gives a little tap-dance.

I look over at a baby blue baby doll dress resting on the bed, my persona for the show. Out of the window, Kristen has gone again, vanished to wherever in the universe her energy has settled.

I slip into the dress ready to be born, knowing deep down that I won't forget this night, likely never ever.

* * * * *

12

• • • • •

Ready to Guide – Grenade Bouquets

The Rusted Nail is down on the Lower East Side, where walk-up buildings meet scuzzy bars and flophouses on Bowery. The streets are narrower filled with music seekers out for the night: punks with green mohawks stuffing into one venue, a flannel shirt crowd spilling out of another, girls in the shortest leather skirts possible with fishnet stockings and combat boots with the laces tied up top, struggling to light a cigarette in the drizzling rain. Taxi cabs honking and homeless huddling under scaffolding and using full garbage bags as pillows. The sound of a million separate conversations congealing. In New York we all become one united organism with a night of debauchery the goal.

We pull up in our van and have to circle the blocks twelve times to find a metered parking spot before giving up and leaving it in a lot near Chinatown. We each carry an instrument to the venue: Ed with two amps under each arm. An actual line snakes outside of the Rusted Nail, an eighteen and over club that will likely look the other way with fake IDs, since half of those waiting are teenagers. Two girls with heavy mascara are hugging one another, whispering. One points my way with a blue fingernail. "She's the one," I hear her say to the other, whose eyes go wide. They soak me in wondering what I have planned for the night. Even I don't know yet.

Inside, is our biggest venue yet. The stage lit with multi-colored lights: pinks, purples, blues and reds creating a prism. The bar is situated at the other end with a Hell's Angel bartender wearing sunglasses indoors and a leather jacket with the sleeves cut off to showcase his muscles. We're the opening band before Shark Invested Waters and then Wheaties, a grunge band from New Jersey who's been around since the late eighties. I've actually heard of them and owned their cassette before Winter broke it one time when she tossed it at me and it cracked on the pavement.

Clarissa and I haven't spoken at all since our last incident. She's become super withdrawn. She wears these Jackie O sunglasses at all hours of the day and has taken to chewing her nails down to the nubs. I think she's been on something, but I'm cool with whatever keeps her quiet and away from me. No one else in the band seems to want to fix our skirmish, since it's entertaining and driving folks to our shows.

At the bar, Evan gets us two Coronas while Lacey and the rest of band sets up and Clarissa disappears into the bathroom. We clink bottles.

"I can't believe this is our last show," I say, not ready to go back to L.A. Summer is ending along with this adventure and school will start. I can't imagine roaming its halls, sitting in class while my leg taps to the beat of one of our songs. Hanging out with Winter and Jeremy after and trying to hold my tongue when sketchy Emily joins. I'll likely wind up punching her sometime. It all seems so immature and part of a different lifetime. I know I told the 'rents I'd be back at school in the fall, but without Evan, without singing, what's the point of existing?

Evan raises an eyebrow in a sneaky way.

"What?" I ask.

"Just been thinking," he says, and takes a sudsy sip. "What if we booked some more shows?"

The feedback from the amp assaults our ears, and we hear Ed saying, "Sorry, sorry."

"I want to be wherever you are," I say, focusing on the beer attached to his lip. I kiss it and taste what he just tasted. I can't imagine not be able to do that whenever I want. The distance between California and Oregon grueling, unfair, criminal.

***

We do a run-through of "Ready to Guide", with the band aping the beat we gave to Ace of Base's "The Sign". It works great and Ed and Randy congratulate me on the song. Lacey finds it brooding and meaningful, the Mazzy Star-ish-meets-Smashing Pumpkins-meets-Nirvana sound the Bouquets are aiming for. Clarissa smokes her cigarette on the edge of the stage while we play, the zigzagging smoke oozing from her lips. Her eyes would be judging if they weren't behind huge sunglasses. She gives all of two claps when we finish and hammers her point home even more with a casual yawn.

"What?" I ask, stomping over to her.

"Who am I to give an opinion?" she says, to the air. "I'm barely a singer anymore."

"Clarissa, that's not true," Ed says, flipping his bass guitar over his shoulder.

"No, I can see it," she says, ashing her cigarette on the stage. "Here I am just sitting here. The band plays on, like I never existed."

"We all play a part," Evan says, as he pinches the bridge of his nose. I'm squealing inside because it means he's over her b.s. city.

"I don't think that's the case anymore, but okay." She uncrosses her legs and rises. "I'll play nice-nice for tonight. I'll close this out like a professional."

She saunters backstage to where we've left some of our stuff. I follow her, not really knowing why. She's in front of a dirty mirror with her makeup kit out.

"You can have him," she says, into the mirror. She puckers as she puts on pink lipstick. "I haven't been into him in a long time."

"I don't need your permission."

I see myself in the mirror as well, a smaller version than her because of where I'm standing.

"But you won't take this band away from me, you child." She swivels around and knocks into my shoulder. It hurts but I pretend like it doesn't. "Not over my dead and tortured body."

She slinks into the shadows and is gone. I go up to the dirty mirror to fix my own makeup. Give a touch-up to my lipstick and go a little wild with the rouge. Make my hair stand up in electrocuted spears. Raccoon eyes with a touch of blue eye shadow to match my hair. I give a rip down my dress like I've been in a fight. My nail polish perfectly peeling. Take a picture of me— I'm ready. Take a picture of this girl about to become a woman.

***

The band sounds more sublime than ever before. Maybe it's the lights or the swell of the crowd. They've packed themselves in; the teenagers and the punks, the partiers and the lost and disillusioned. They sway like pendulums during our ballads, they destroy themselves during our rock songs. The mosh pit is its own island with many little tornados. They are all scarred and bleeding but pleased, pure again. They came into the Rusted Nail angry at their parents, or their boyfriends and girlfriends, or their teachers, or their siblings, or the kids at school that shove them in lockers. Our music is their salvation and they eat it up like a Christ wafer. They let it simmer in their stomachs and flow through their veins, electrifying their movements. They are creatures of the night out for blood, and even more than that, to be understood. They find solace in our words, in our licks from "Disarm" to "Into Your Arms" to my banshee cry of Hole's "Violet". To Clarissa and I making our throats sore as we belt out Courtney Love's gorgeous anguish. For a moment we are not enemies, but champions. We have a goal to take the audience through this journey, to rock their souls, to shake them to the core, and leave them upended with a little piece of our bliss. I'm singing as if it's the last time I will ever sing, as if my throat will close forever afterwards, my final peep on this Earth, for them, for Kristen, for me, for that little girl who never thought she'd have the ability to be in front of a crowd.

The prism lights flash as the song builds to its shattering conclusion. I'm bathed in a glow, my baby blue dress and my blue hair blue like the ocean. I'm swimming. I'm ashore. The multi-colored lights unify to one strobe painting me in the middle of the stage. The band recedes into the darkness as I wrap my arms around the mic stand like it's my lover. The guitar beats are low, the drum muted but powerful, my whisper becomes a rage as I sing, "Ready to Guide."

> *Your ghost remains inside*
> *Ready to guide*
> *Your ghost remains inside*
> *Ready to guide*

The song could be a B-side from Hole, could've been written with Courtney Love's bloody quill. It could've been a track that Nirvana never got to record, or one that Billy Corgan wished he did, or Chris Cornell thought he had, or Eddie Vedder dreamed, or Scott Weiland sang to a lover in bed, but it's all mine. From deep within the places in my body where sadness dwells and sticks, released into the ears of whoever is here to listen to it come to life. It stalks around the venue, this earworm, it burrows inside until it's lodged in your brain.

> *Scars have healed*
> *Wounds no longer appeal*

You've brought out my voice
And I've made the right choice

If Kristen is listening, I'm singing loud enough for the acoustics in heaven to pick up my timbre. She can tuck her ear against a cloud as the words float upwards.

But for now, sadness has no appeal
Because your ghost remains inside
Ready to guide
Your ghost remains inside
Ready to Guide

The lights begin flashing like they're having a seizure. The mosh pit has slowed but still holds onto to its threat, people colliding into one another like bumper cars to the beat. A sea of eyes enraptured as I bring the song to a close, our last song, possibly forever, our final stake. Their applause envelopes me. It takes so long for it to die down. They want more. They are demanding. We are not finished, but Shark Invested Waters need to come on.

"We are Grenade Bouquets," I say, with a fistful of tears trapped in my throat. "Thank you for listening."

If that's the last they hear of me, I have to be satisfied with what I've given them. I rush off the stage before anyone in the band can console. I'm standing at the fringe, sweat pouring from my face but shivering at the same time. A man hovers over me. He's got slicked-back salt and pepper hair. His teeth are perfectly white. He's in a sleek suit with a thin black tie. No one else is wearing a suit here. He's an alien.

"You were great," he says, over the din of the music still piercing.

I can't speak. I'm not ready. I try to nod at him but tears obscure my eyes.

"Your original song. That was the highlight. See these goosebumps?" He rolls up his sleeve and sure enough they're there. "Still got them. That's rare."

The frog leaves my throat and I manage to murmur, "Thank you."

"Thank *you*." He holds out his hand: manicured fingernails, bracelets in gold and silver.

"I'm Terry Carbon," he says, his accent veering Australian.

"N-Nico."

My palm is a sweat pit, but I shake his.

"Nico Sullivan," he says, out of the corner of his mouth. "I heard. And you're Grenade Bouquets. I saw your write-up in Guitar Picks. I wanted to come to your show."

"It's our last show," I say, as if the fate of the world has ended.

"I'm the A&R man at Grouch Records. You're just the sound that we're looking for."

"What...?" I ask, because Shark Invested Waters have started up and they're loud enough to split our eardrums.

"I said, I think you can be huge. You, girl. Your band."

He's shouting and he whips off his sunglasses and these tiny pupils stare back, reading my every move. I feel like I'm going faint, so I leap into his arms instead with a yodel, fist to the sky, stamping my Doc Martins, shrieking loud enough for the other side of the world to hear. He's cackling and we're dancing around as the rest of the band comes over perplexed. I'm the first one to share the news.

"We're gonna be stars," I say, falling into my drunkenness. The many beers sloshing around. All I've imbibed since this tour began. That's helped formed me into this chanteuse, like it or not. "The biggest and brightest in the night," I say, with flare.

And I picture us, hanging out in the Milky Way, shimmering with all of our might.

Ready to guide whoever needs our pulsation.

13

• • • • • •

Dreams – The Cranberries

We stay at the Rusted Nail having drinks with Terry Carbon who puts it all on his tab. He talks about the power of female-fronted bands in the grunge market-place. He says this all to me and not Clarissa. She hovers, trying to get a word in, but he's laser focused. He rattles off some of his favorites: Heavens to Betsy, Hole, L7, The Breeders. The future is women. That's who Cobain would want to hand the torch to, like he did to his wife. "That's you," he says, and the band all nods, but he's speaking directly to me. I'm the next Kim Deal. I'm the next Courtney Love.

At around midnight, Terry Carbon tells us he's got an early morning and gives us his card to set up a demo recording of "Ready to Guide".

"We'll start with that and go from there," he says, with a snap of fingers. He puts on John Lennon sun-glasses and walks out into the night. The band discusses about extending our motel stay through the week at least while we record. I'm expected home and need to figure out a way to convince the 'rents. School starts up in just over a week, and I gotta prepare my court case.

"We're getting shots," Ed yells over to me. "Fuzzy Navels." He signals for the muscled bartender.

"I should make a call."

Evan pulls me close, our noses touching. "Where you going?"

"I wanna…call my aunt Carly."

He cocks his head to the side. "Now?"

"It's only nine p.m. in Ojai." I'm pulling away from him, but he's nuzzling my neck.

"Stay. Hang with us. I'm so excited, Nico."

He's slurring his words; the band is all on their way to getting super blasted.

"If I'm gonna be able to do all this, I need her to help convince my parents."

"Convince them to do what?"

We're yelling over The Meat Puppets' "Backwater" blasting from the speakers on the ceiling.

"School starts soon. Like, I'll be missing the first day."

He looks at me strange and then nods his head. "Right, high school."

"Right. High school. I can't not just show up. Anyway, lemme call her."

I slip out of his grasp and make my way outside. There's a phone booth at the end of the street and I feed it quarters and dial Carly's number.

"Yes? Hello?" Carly says.

Right now, part of me needs to hear the voice of someone who knows me well. The last few hours have been overwhelming to say the least. I just sang the best show of my short life and now we're recording a demo! It's too much to comprehend.

"Carly, it's me."

"Hey, Nico." I can hear her smiling. Carly's voice always has a sweet lilt, likely from the glass of red wine probably in her hand, but also because she lived her life in as positive a way as possible. That's what was so different between her and my parents. They would yell at my choices while she would cheer me on.

I go through everything that happened in a rush of verbal diarrhea. I'm talking so fast I can barely understand it myself. Taking Carly city by city through our tour until it culminated in New York.

"Wow, Nico, a demo!" I hear her making kissy noises. "C'mere, Gussy, Nico's got some news."

"Hi, Gus," I say, to one of her many cats.

"And this guy, he's legit?"

I take out Terry Carbon's card. A&R at Grouch Records. The card crisp and white, the stock heavy, with images of records along the trim.

"Yeah, he's from Grouch Records. They're like huge. But...school starts in over a week."

"Hmmm," she says.

"This is my dream, Carly. Like how many people get to live their dream?"

"Nico, I'm going to tell you this only once, and that is - this train is already in motion. Everything you've done has led up to this moment, do you understand that?"

The phone is shaking in my hand as this oracle continues her proclamation.

"Now, I dropped out of school so my opinion

on it will vary from your parents. But I didn't have a reason when I dropped out. Did I, Gussy?" I hear her making kissy noises to her cat again. "And you do. Not that I'm advocating dropping out. But you *have* to record this demo."

"Yeah, that's what I'm thinking."

"If I know your father, he won't understand. Peter has always had a business mind. That man doesn't have an ounce of creativity in him. I will help you make them understand."

"Oh, Carly, thank you. I mean, you're like the only adult I feel I can rely on."

"Just make sure to dedicate one of your songs to your old aunt. Your old dotty aunt. Oh, Nico, I'm so proud." She sniffles.

"Are you crying, Carly?"

"Uh-huh, I am. My sweet girl."

Now I'm crying too and the two of us are drunkenly bawling our eyes out. I don't even realize how sloshed I am.

"When you came to me last spring, oh, Nico, you were so, so broken. Your sister, the tragedy…"

"I know, I know."

"You weren't shining. You were dim. And I wondered when you would get that light back inside of you. I knew you would because life is long and we're built to get over tragedies. We have too. But I thought you would be hurting for so long. And then, you returned a few weeks later, with a boy, a very nice boy, and you had sung, you had sung, my baby, and your face just lit up when you described it. Oh, it warmed my heart, child. To see that light within you again."

"I feel it, I do."

"There's no way that I will let that light go out of you again. Let me decide how to broach your father about this. We'll be a united front."

I'm gushing, my love for the woman indescribable. "Thank you, thank you so much."

"Okay, Nico, you have my blessing. Go enjoy yourself tonight. Celebrate for your old, dotty aunt."

I hang up after saying I loved her, confident that we would be able to convince my parents that this is what I had to do. I make my way back to the bar where The Cranberries' "Dreams" is blasting from the speakers like it's narrating a soundtrack to my life.

"I requested it," Evan says, and kisses me on the ear.

We all sing along to the song, arm-in-arm, even Clarissa who's drunk enough to match our revelry. We sing about our life changing every day, every possible way. Our dreams. Our dreams.

Whatever happens from here on out, this would be a moment I'll come back to, when the future gaped wide open for us, and there were no mines in sight to potentially explode it all to pieces.

Yet.

14

• • • • • •

Something in the Way – Nirvana

We're in a fancy recording studio and I haven't eaten breakfast because I was afraid I might throw it all up, so I just sucked down coffee and now I've hella got the jitters like mad. It's one thing to sing on stage, to lose yourself in the lights and the sway of the crowd, it's another to have all eyes on me while I try to hit the right note in a booth. Terry Carbon wears his John Lennon sunglasses inside and there's a few others from Grouch Records who he introduced me to but I forget who they are. The band is setting up their instruments and Clarissa's getting into her own groove by stretching her mouth and speaking all the vowels in a pronounced way. The radio is on faintly and Nirvana's "Something in the Way" plays, as if it was there to remind me of my former idol and how this wild adventure began. *This is for you, Cobain*, I tilt my head back and whisper like he might be trapped in the ceiling observing.

"So, we're just gonna do one song today and go from there," Terry Carbon says. He has a way of speaking where his thin lips and long tongue made him look like a lizard.

The Grouch Records people whisper in his ear and he points at me. "Just with you."

"Me?" I ask, and swivel my head around looking flummoxed.

"Ready to Guide," he says, with a whistle at the end of his voice. "That's the one we'll do. Meaning…" He beckons at Clarissa, who shuts up her vowel exercises and gets concerned lines along her forehead as she squints. "Sweetheart, yeah, you sweetheart, with the hair."

Clarissa touches her hair, embarrassed.

"Yeah, let's have you sit out for this one."

Clarissa combs the long locks of her hair on one side, her fingers yanking at the split ends like she was imagining digging into my soul.

"But I'm the singer," she says, only a peep. Her power already diminishing.

Terry Carbon and the suits around him catch each other's eye.

"Clarissa, it's Nico's song," Evan says, focusing on tuning his guitar. Ed and Randy have nothing to add, staying Switzerland.

We all enter the booth and Clarissa is left outside stewing with her elbows on her knees and her chin in her palm. I'd feel bad for her, but she honestly brought this upon herself.

It's certainly a challenge recording as opposed to singing on stage. We have a few false starts, the band playing a little too fast for me to jump in. I lose my place a few times. When Terry Carbon beckons me, I get a sour taste in my mouth. I take off my headphones and meet him outside in a hallway where he leans in close.

"Sweetheart, are you nervous?"

Apparently, we're all sweethearts.

"No, I..."

"It's okay if you are. This is new, right? A brand-new experience. Well, so what's the solution?" He snaps his fingers. "What inspired this song?"

"My-my sister died."

Saying it was like sticking my hand into murky waters and trying to retrieve something special I lost. I'd hadn't even thought about Kristen today. That was beginning to happen more and more, as if she'd never even existed.

Terry Carbon blew the bangs from his eyes. I could tell he had no idea how to respond. He snapped his fingers again.

"We'll use that. I mean, you know what I mean. Use what you're feeling. Go deep. Don't be afraid to be gnarly."

Back in the booth, I channeled the last time I sang the song to Kristen. When I was in the graveyard previewing it for her. I closed my eyes, not needing to read the lyrics since I knew them from my heart. Terry Carbon and the other Grouch Records folks fell away, even the rest of Grenade Bouquets. I was no longer thinking about how Clarissa felt, or Ed, Randy or Evan either. All that existed was the music flowing from their instruments. I injected it into to my veins and began to sing, making my voice throatier than usual with a growl like I was chewing on the words as if they were a tough piece of steak.

This train doesn't need to run away
I'm on the right pathway

Kristen's watching me perform. She's whole and beautiful again, full of life.

Your ghost remains inside
Ready to guide

I pause for an instrumental break where the band noodles around while I'm moving to the beats with a snake-like wriggle.

So it'll never be good-bye
Only till next time

There are tears shooting down my cheeks, sticky and hot in the airless studio. I'm nearing the end of the song, fighting with my voice not to break, pouring true emotion into the mic.

And when I'm old and done
And my time has come
We can reunite for real
But for now, sadness has no appeal

I'm ready for the final chorus, to bring up all that's been festering inside of me related to Kristen's death. I've gotten so much better ever since my runaway, but some of it remains. It always will. I think of all the kids who will be listening, those who lost loved ones and are looking to this song for guidance. I am their torch through the darkness.

Because your ghost remains inside

Ready to guide
Ready to guide

I hold the final note for as long as I can, through eons of despair until I release. The band plays a few more chords until only the reverberations can be heard trapped in the air. I open my eyes and the band is staring back at me shocked, all of us shaking like we created something major and don't know how to put it into words yet. We're vibrating on another level. We've ascended.

Terry Carbon and his people are grinning wide enough to show me their back molars. He begins to clap breaking the silence. They turn to each other with affirmative nods.

"I think we have a hit on our hands," he says, with a throwback laugh.

And I allow myself to smile because I felt it deep inside too. That nothing in my life from here on out would ever be the same.

15

• • • • •

Feel the Pain – Dinosaur Jr.

The short of it is, Grouch Records lurvs our demo and wants to sign us for a full album. They believe we'll be a bridge between the old grunge bands and a new sound emerging with an upcoming generation. At least that's the speak we've been told. I'm hella jazzed but not surprised after our recording sesh. I could tell we impressed Terry Carbon and the others. The band goes to celebrate even though it's during the day and I'm still sleeping off the hangover from last night. We went hard then, and in the foggy light of the morning, I'm regretting all the shots I did, promising myself I'll be better at turning them down in the future. So, I'm left alone in the motel room and listening to my mixtape. "Feel the Pain" by Dinosaur Jr. is pumping through my headphones, and I'm smoking a cigarette, which has become a new habit of mine, while ashing into a tray in the shape of girl sitting in a large martini glass with the olive covering up her unmentionables. I call the 'rents, first my mom, and then we do three-way call.

"Carly spoke to us last night," was all Dad said, curt and to the point.

I'm wrapping the phone cord around my index finger and realizing I need to reapply my blue nail polish. "Oh, did she?"

"Nico, we can't in good faith—" Mom interrupts.

"Luanne, let me handle this."

"I will not, Peter. We need to be a unified front."

They're both arguing and not making much sense, so I turn up the volume on my Sports Walkman and sing the chorus to myself until they're done.

"You are not dropping out," they both decide.

"No, I'm not dropping out," I say. "And it's not just a demo, the record company wants us to record a whole album. Do you get what that means?"

This shuts them up. For a sec at least.

"How much are you getting paid?" Dad asks, always concerned about cashola more than anything else. This would be my way in.

"Our manager Lacey is negotiating right now, but it's a lot. Like, a lot, a lot."

"Give me a ballpark," Dad says.

So, I tell him the figure, which honestly is crazy to say out loud, and now they're so quiet all I hear is breathing over the phone.

"Luanne, that's a lot of money," Dad finally says, and Mom squawks in response.

"Peter, don't let her convince you—"

"Convince what?" I butt in. "Convince you that I've found something in my life I'm really good at, which I have the potential to *actually* make money off of. I can take a G.E.D, I can still get a degree. It's not like

I had such amazing grades that colleges were foaming at the mouth to take me."

"That's true," Peter says.

"I can take this semester off. To record the album and then we can reassess from there," I say, proud of myself for speaking so eloquently and calmly. "If I don't do this, I'll always look back and regret it for like for the rest of my life."

"But where will you stay?" Mom asks.

I have no idea but make up a lie about the girls getting a place and the guys in a separate one. That Lacey has family connections who can get us a deal. It's believable enough for Mom to move on to another worry.

"But New York City," she says, and I can hear the shiver in her voice. Derelicts on every corner, drugs rampant, muggers abound. It's not like L.A. is any better, it's just that the L.A. she frequents is far enough away from its rough edges.

"You're only seventeen."

I go into a speech about great women in history who all did amazing and super important things before they turned eighteen.

"In another year I'll be able to vote, join the army, like I should be fine in a walk-up in downtown New York City."

"Peter, I don't like how she convinced us this easily," Mom says.

"Does that mean you're convinced?" I ask.

"No, it does not," Mom says, but I can tell by Dad's silence that he is.

"Let her record the album, Luanne, and we can go from there," Dad says, and Mom starts to say more, but then out of exhaustion, or realizing she won't win this battle, gives in.

"Sweetie, I don't like this," she says, as if she needs that declaration to be noted. She's still afraid of what happened to me after Kristen died, dancing on eggshells. I needed to use that to my advantage.

"I should go, we have to get to work," I say, even though I know that "work" has consisted of the band getting major shitty at a dumpy bar on the corner.

After I hang up with them, I call Winter. Her mom picks up first. I recycle the latest news and allow myself to bask in Edina's adulations.

"Oh, Nico, this is so fantastic," she says, and I can hear sucking at a joint.

"Thanks, Edina," I say. "It's all happened so quickly."

"Soak it up, that's my advice." The crackle from the joint amplifies through the receiver, sounding like crumpling tinfoil. "I had designs to sing once."

"Really?" I lie back and place my feet against the wall. There's a crack in shape of Florida.

"When Joplin was so big, I bloody longed to be just like her. I would drink Scotch from a bottle, poof my hair like her, wear the same shades."

I think of how I've been doing that with Courtney Love as of late.

"But I never had the pipes for anything serious. No, it's just singing in the bath for me. But you, Nico…"

I'm blushing.

"Don't forget about the little people in your life."

"Never. Is Winter there?"

There's an odd silence before she responds, as if she knows about the issues Winter and I have had. Edina and her are so close that I can't imagine she hasn't shared anything, probably making me out to be the enemy in every situation, even when she's to blame.

"Let me get her," Edina says, in a warm way that lets me understand she'll be on my side, or at least stay neutral.

"Hello," Winter says, after a click.

"Niiiiiicooooo," I hear Jeremy shout.

Weird music pumps from Winter's speakers that I assume must be Marilyn Manson. I hear the phone being tossed and Jeremy picks up.

"Hey, Nico Rico Suave."

"Hey, Jer, where's Winter?"

"She's...uh...dyeing her hair."

I remember giving that excuse to the 'rents when I didn't want to talk to them.

"Really?"

"Yeah, no she is," he says. "Give her a minute."

I tell Jeremy all the deets about recording an album and not returning to school.

"Wait, girl, what? Who will I make fun of everyone with if you won't be there?"

"I think I convinced the 'rents."

"Wow, Nico, hella props. I never thought Luanne would just let you move in with your boyfriend."

It hadn't occurred to me that Evan and I would be living together. I pictured us learning each other's morning habits. How he liked his coffee. The side of bed he preferred. The taste of him before toothpaste would hit his teeth.

"Can you talk?" I hear Jeremy call over to Winter. I don't hear what she says, if she's making up some excuse to avoid my ass.

"Please put her on," I say, embarrassed that I sound like I'm begging. Jeremy covers the receiver end of the phone, and I know he's trying to convince her. Finally, Winter picks up again.

"I really am in mid-dye."

"Is Emily there?" I ask, but what I really want to say is *I miss you.*

"She had something to take care of at home," Winter says. "So, you're recording an album?"

She says this as if it's practically meaningless. The Winter I used to know would've gone apeshit.

"Yeah, like an actual contract with real money. The record company loves our demo. It's Grouch Records, they rep the Pogo Sticks and the Slitters."

"Yeah, yeah I know."

"O…kay, well, so I'm not coming back to school, at least for now."

"That's intense," she says, although the way she says it, she makes it clear that it's not.

"I mean, maybe I'll get a G.E.D., I dunno. But we're all gonna find a place in the city while we make an album. And who knows how long it'll take."

"Who knows?"

"I mean, it's an expression, like…"

She turns up the Marilyn Manson screeching.

"Winter, I can barely hear you."

"I love this song," she says, and starts singing, or really growling, along.

"I know, but I can't hear—"

"It's art," she says, as if she's giving me a dig, as if what I'm creating is purely for dough and nothing else.

"Are you jealous or something?"

Immediately, I want to eat those words, however much they might be true. The music gets turned down and I hear Winter hiss, "Jeremy, leave."

"I'm gonna make Pizza rolls," Jeremy says, before I hear a door slam.

"Jealous, Nico? You think I'm jealous?"

"I ... I don't know how to talk to you anymore." The truth bombs coming out of my mouth are making me shake with nerves. I'm afraid that we're going in a direction with this conversation I'll never be able to veer from.

"Because you're *so* high and mighty." She makes a huffing sound. "Honestly, Nico, ever since you came back from your runaway extravaganza you've been insufferable."

Count to ten, I say to myself, over and over before I might decide to explode on her.

"I found something that I love to do, Winter. And that I'm good at. And like, just be excited for me."

"What about all the amazing things I've been doing?" Her voice is like cut glass.

"Okay, tell me. I wanna hear!"

"No, you don't. You just want to talk about yourself. Like the world revolves around you."

"That's not true." I'm eating my tears now. "Winter, this is the biggest thing that's happened to me."

"I met this guy, okay. He's like older, he used to go to our school. Anyway, it's getting serious."

"Was this from that party at Emily's house?"

"This has nothing to do with Emily. You don't have to be jealous of her."

"I'm not, I just thought you met him at her pool party."

"No, we met before, in fact we had sex like a long time ago and he rocked my world. Anyway, you're not the only one quitting school, I am too."

"But why? For what? For this guy?"

"He has a motorcycle, Nico, and we're gonna like ride on it. Edina already knows, she's cool with it. Like, senior year is so lame. Everyone's gonna be applying to colleges, and I'm like so not into that. I'm done."

"Are you gonna get a G.E.D.?"

"Girl, get off my dick. I dunno. We're gonna ride up the PCH and see where that takes us. Like, he's a real man, not like that skinny boy you're with who I could break. Not Don. Don's got long locks of hair and like so many tattoos. He's got this tattoo of a skull on his chest and like the skull is eating blood, it's so fucking hot. And we do it without condoms…"

"What? Winter, really?"

"Yes, really because we're in love and like if I get preggers, I get preggers. We've talked about a family and me being a bride, like the ripped dress I'd wear. He's told me he loves me."

"How old is he?"

"I said he's a real man. He's twenty-three. I mean, he went to our school, but not when we were there. He's been in jail, like everything about him makes me moist."

I gulp. "Jail?"

"It was like a dumb bar fight, at least the first time. Second was auto theft, but not really. He loves Marilyn Manson too. We're gonna see him on tour."

"Edina is really okay with all of this?"

"Yes, Suzy Square, you know she lets me do what I want. And like *this* is what I want. Emily's seeing this guy whose Don's friend and has a bike too, so we're gonna be biker chicks. They call us their old ladies."

"When are you leaving? And Jeremy knows? I mean, who's he gonna have to hang with?"

"Yeah, I haven't broken it to Jer yet, but Jer loves me unconditionally unlike you, and he'll just be happy for me."

"I am happy for you."

"No, you're judging. I can hear it in your voice."

Had my voice betrayed me? I want to be happy for her, but everything about this screams *bad idea*.

"I'm shocked—"

"So see? We have lives and exciting things happening to us as well. It's not only the Nico show."

"I never said it was."

"So like, record your album, and live with your boyfriend who's a budget K.C., and don't worry about your girl Winter. She always lands on both her feet."

"How will I be in touch with you? I mean…" My voice goes small. "Do you even want me to be in touch with you?"

Silence on her end. It stings and then whips, abuses.

"I got a beeper."

She reels off the number and I grab a motel pen and scribble it on my palm.

"Okay." I take a deep breath. "I'm excited for you, Winter, if this is what you want. Please just make sure you're safe."

"I plan to eat cyanide the whole time."

"Really, just...be safe."

"You be safe, Suzy Square."

"I lov—"

"I gotta go, Nico, Jer's coming back with the pizza rolls and I *can't* have this convo with him right now."

"Oh, okay, bye—"

"Tootles, bitch."

The phone clicks. I hang up, my feet still planted against the wall. I'm nauseous from the hangover and a dread feeling for Winter. I grab my Walkman and start up where I left off, "Feel the Pain" by Dinosaur Jr. I turn it up loud, burning my vocal cords, feeling the pain of everyone: Winter and myself even more. How it feels to have a best friend slipping away, knowing there's nothing I can do to keep her close, keep her mine.

16

• • • • •

In Circles – Sunny Day Real Estate

Grouch Records splurges for a basement apartment for us on Essex Street. They call it a railroad style, each room bleeding into the next, culminating in a chamber where we make our music. There's a mini stage there and room for Randy's drums. Evan's always noodling on his guitar, lyrics coming from his dreams. We're all inspired. We don't sleep. It's hard to tell whose room is whose. The apartment only has tiny slivers of windows by the ceilings. We see people's feet as they walk on by, except for my bedroom that gets a full window. We emerge to go to the bodega down the block and live off of those orange Hostess cupcakes and Dipsy Doodles. If we're feeling daring, we make eggs. The record company provides us with copious amounts of pot, beautiful green buds to get our synapses firing. We have jugs of vodka, top shelf tequila, a fridge full of beer bottles. They offer us whatever we want. It's not only suggested, it's encouraged. We are their stars.

I've taken to writing little flicks of poems down my

arms. The rest goes into a journal I clutch like a child's blankie. We listen to a lot of Sunny Day Real Estate. Mazzy Star. The Smashing Pumpkins' earlier records like *Gish*. Nirvana's B-sides. Stone Temple Pilots' *Purple*. Sonic Youth. Soundgarden's *Superunknown* with its blurry screaming face on the cover. Nine Inch Nails' *The Downward Spiral* and "Closer" over and over, of course Hole's *Live Through This* and Pearl Jam's *Vitology*. Live's *Throwing Copper* with its piercing "Lightning Crashes" and "I Alone". Bush's *Sixteen Stone* and its torturous "Glycerine". *What is glycerine?* we ask and decide *it doesn't matter.* Veruca Salt and Belly's "Feed the Tree", Liz Phair and The Meat Puppets, Soul Asylum's "Can't Even Tell", Sponge's "Plowed" and "Molly", Bad Religion, and lots and lots of Alice in Chains further on into the night when we're too tired to keep our heads up. We start to record. Inklings of songs. A melody. We need to be in sync. We all sleep in the same bed one night so our dreams can coalesce. Evan's foot winds up by my face and in the middle of the night, I pull off his stinky sock and kiss his big toe. The nail is surprisingly manicured, the toe tasting like sweet milk.

> *Big toe, big toe*
> *How I love you so*
> *You taste of sweet milk*
> *My lips like silk*

I start singing out loud. It's three a.m. and so dark in that room I can't see anything. A laser blue night cutting over my bandmates' faces. It dances over Evan's. His fine blond fuzz of a beard. He sleeps so soundly, like he has no worries.

Your quiet sleep
My demon head
You have no worries
I dream of dead.

I tickle his foot and he wakes. Flops away Randy's arm and sits up.

"Hey," he mouths to me.

I gesture to the door and we're in the hallway. I haven't fully slept in days, unsure if I'm awake or still in a dream.

Big toe, big toe
How I love you so

"Is that our new song?" he asks, smirking.

"I love you," I say in my head, and melt in his arms. Maybe he puts me to sleep on the couch. Brushes my hair from my face. Stays with me until morning.

I'm surrounded by the band getting loaded at the crack of light. Whiskey stains on the coffee table. The air thick with cigarettes. We all smoke a pack a day. Evan picks up his guitar and a tune falls out. It's dark and mysterious, the strumming angry. Randy follows along. Evan's singing about his brother, a tweak on the original song, a scathing shot at George Bush for Desert Storm, how its soldiers were left behind when they returned home. The last line just says, Norman Schwarzkoff. Another day, I'm singing about going around in circles never reaching a destination and we wind up in our music chamber and another song is born. The next day I wake up and I'm crying about Kristen, which still happens even though it's way less than before, and we have a song called "Drowning", parts of it sketched over my arms. That night we smoke from a gravity bong and create "Lasso", about the lengths we go through to keep a girlfriend or boyfriend entertained. In the morning, I'm making eggs and "Sunny Side Down" is born, inspired by Ed's father who's been in and out of rehab. "Charlie" is our take on "Jeremy" about a kid being bullied at school who retaliates. "See-Saw" flirts with bulimia, after hearing Lacey's story when she was thirteen. "Split" is about Randy dealing with liking both men and women. "Hole in the Bucket" deals with suicide, and all the ways we've flirted with it in thought and in practice. I remember during my runaway last year when I took a pill and got behind the wheel. How I wanted to crash. How I wanted a pain greater than I was experiencing inside. We've all lived long lives during our short ones and the album would be an ode to our generation. Not Generation X, we're too young. We're not them. We're something new. And we do not want to be forgotten.

When we're not recording, we tell each other our stories. Besides Evan, they only knew a little about Kristen, so I open up. What her death has done to me. How it's also helped me to soar. The addiction in Ed's family brings him to tears. This giant bear of a man weeping like a lost kid. He's seen his dad inject between his toes. No one expects rehab to work anymore but it's just what you do. Randy tells of the first man he fell in love with. A cop in Boston with a thick accent. How he was afraid to go into a gay bar and walked past the entrance a thousand times before he forced himself inside. This cop who drank rum and Cokes and crunched on the ice. How it felt to kiss him for the first time in an alleyway and that he was surprised by the scruff on his cheeks. How women were never as interesting since then. And with Evan, how he finds himself thinking about Evan, cursing himself but unable to stop. Evan goes over and kisses him on the forehead. I know that little bit of contact is even worse than nothing at all. Evan returns to my arms and I see murder in Randy's eyes. I look across the room and see murder in Clarissa's as well.

She tells a story about trying to kill herself. She shows us her wrists. Normally she wears long sleeves, and I never thought about why. She pulls down the sleeves and there are two horizontal scars along her wrists.

"I didn't do it the right way," she says, as if it's a joke. She gives a sheepish grin and mimes how to do it, vertically along the vein. Evan looks down because he knows this story. He cares for her when she's vulnerable, and I can't blame him.

"I wanted someone to notice me." She's not smiling anymore, her mouth a black hole. "Like no one noticed me in high school. It was this preppy hell. Everyone in their sweater sets. I was the malevolent spirit on campus, flitting amongst the shadows. Was I even there? Anyway, I did it one day when the bell rang. So, it would be the first thing they would all see when they stepped inside. One girl screamed so loud I can still hear it. She never came back to school. I did. Eventually. They taped up my wrists. Easier to pretend it never happened than truly deal with the consequences. My parents ate their ambrosia salad like it never happened. We never once spoke of it. I never speak to them anymore."

We let her go on because she hadn't talked much since we began the recording sessions. I'd catch her watching Evan and I, her eye appearing in a crack in the door. She kept to her room mostly, lighting candles and eternally sipping from a bottle of bourbon. She'd emerge to pee or sometimes harmonize with us. She sang on every song when we'd record, but she was an after-thought, all of us knowing her true place in the band, waiting for it to be official. I heard her one night arguing with Evan. It must have been four in the morning and they were on the street so not to wake us up. The fight came down through the little window in the kitchen with the metal bars. She was apologizing for cheating on him. That sex shouldn't define a relationship. That it was meaningless. They had something. Truly something and he threw it away.

"That was a long time ago," he said.

"No, it wasn't."

"It was to me."

"You left me stranded."

"You did that to yourself."

"Nico ruined everything."

An imaginary knife stabs me in the gut at the mention of my name. I'm both titillated and scared, awaiting his reply.

Big toe, big toe

How I love you so

He comes back in the apartment, sees me lurking. I've become Clarissa.

"I'm sorry you had to hear that," he says, kicking at the wall.

"I am too."

He rubs his eyes until they're raw.

"What if…" I get excited at mentioning my suggestion, my heart full. "What if we did the band without her?"

He chews his lip, kicks the wall again.

"She started it with us, it would be, like, wrong."

I'm watching to see if Clarissa is coming back inside. There's a light rain and she's standing outside frozen, not caring if she's getting wet.

"We don't need her."

I turn on my charms. I slink over to him, cup his chin, kiss his lips. I'm grinding against him when she returns. He breaks away, fixes his hair, but she stalks right to her room and slams the door.

"Terry Carbon won't care if she's gone," I say, surprised by my deceitfulness. But am I really being deceitful? We have an album to record and if she's getting in the way, well… What are we gaining by keeping her around?

"How do you know that?" he asks, innocent.

"I know," I say, because I will tell Terry Carbon. I'll cut out this cancer. I'll leave Clarissa wounded on the side of the road.

Evan and I finish a bottle of Wild Turkey that night and I sing him "Big Toe". He's laughing again and I realize Clarissa isn't a thought. He picks up his guitar and plays a tune to "Big Toe" that fits perfectly, a sweet ditty to close out the album, a sun beaming on the horizon after so much darkness. We've all suffered, are still suffering. The record reflects that, but there's hope, there's "Big Toe". We record the song and make love as the rain ramps up. When we wake it's still raining, the sky full of grey clouds, no sun in the room, so we stay in bed and drink some more, until day switches to night without us even noticing. I get out of bed and my limbs hurt from not standing for so long. They crack and ache as I slouch to the kitchen and make a sunny side down egg, eating it over the sink while Sunny Day Real Estate's "In Circles" blares from the next room. I get a shiver at the thought that we've finished our album and are about to hella explode.

17

• • • • •

Creep – Radiohead

"Terry Carbon please," I say over the phone, in my best, most adult voice possible.

"One minute," his receptionist says, a perky girl whose nose and eye rings defy her personality.

I'm doing this from a phone booth so there's no chance I could be overheard. I'm shady like that. But it's time for some, time for some action. Clarissa has long overstayed her welcome—

"Hi, Nico, what's the good word?"

Terry Carbon always sounds like he's crawling out of a bender, and I can relate, because I went hard with Johnny Walker last night. We all did, as evidenced by the many empties I dragged out to the trash this morning. Oh well, I'm over chastising myself about it. It's just what rockstars do.

"I need to be honest," I say. There's a bum outside of the phone booth gesturing something. I don't know if he wants money or wants to use to the phone. I turn so I'm not facing him, my mouth flush against the cool receiver. "It's Clarissa."

There's a moment of silence, and I get squirmy. Is he about to disagree with me—I can't tell? But then I realize something even better. He doesn't know who I'm talking about.

"Come again?"

"The other singer? Clarissa?"

I can hear him slapping his forehead. "Right, right."

"She's become..." I hear Radiohead's "Creep" through the phone, playing at a low volume in his office. "Well, she's poison."

"Poison?"

"I mean, she's hurting the band. Really. She used to date Evan and..."

I babble on and on about the trials and tribulations of our Fleetwood Mac drama. Who loves who, who's hating who, and Clarissa at the center of it all.

"Nico," he says, sharply. Enough to get me to stand straight. "Nico, my primary focus is what's best for the band. If she's a problem... We get rid of problems."

"Just like that?"

"Just like that."

My smile takes up my whole face.

"She'll only believe it if she hears it from you." I'm chewing on my lip, worried that I'm pushing my luck, but I'm thrilled at the thought of Terry Carbon giving her the literal boot.

Terry lets out a giant yawn before mumbling, "All right, I'll come over."

I give an internal squeal.

"And how's the album coming along?"

"So, that's the other news. I think we're done."

"You should've led with that."

He hangs up and I rush back to the apartment, cleaning like a madwoman. Everyone's still asleep even though it's past noon. The basement full of cigarette butts everywhere and more empties, which I missed. Leftover food has turned to mush and ants have taken up residence. When the doorbell rings, I'm wiped and need a joint. I throw on a sweatshirt to cover my stained clothes and open the door to Terry Carbon.

He wears a leather jacket even though it's an unseasonably hot end of September. Our block is starting to be littered with yellowed leaves on the ground, a trail to Oz. He removes his shades and gives me three kisses on my cheeks.

"So, this is where the magic happens?" he asks, ducking inside. I see him sniff and wonder if he had a bump or if it's in reference to the smell of the apartment. With only tiny windows, there isn't much chance for air.

I don't know how to respond so I make a face like I'm listening intently for him to say more.

"You changed your hair?"

I touch it in surprise. That's right, I had lost the blue a couple of weeks ago. It's fried blonde now, like La Love.

"Better," he says, twisting a strand around his finger. "We can work with that more. The blue, well, the blue was quite, quite blue." He digs his fists into his leather jacket. "So, I've brought the guillotine."

I squint confused.

"Chop chop, I mean, for our…Clarissa. We've already had a meeting at Grouch. Half of them didn't recall her being in the band. So, it's a non-issue."

"That's great. That's so great."

"Is anyone up?"

"No, most of the time we emerge when the sun goes down."

"Spoken like a true rock band."

He's giving me a smirk and I can't tell if there's an element of flirting on his end, or maybe it's just an Aussie thing. I would never even consider, *never*. Evan and I are doing better than ever. I mean, Clarissa has been a thorn, but it hasn't really affected us. I think of her as the first challenge that we've come across and survived.

"So, point me to her den," he says, and I nod to the first door down the hall. He gives a knock, nothing. He knocks again and then opens the door, disappears inside. I hear murmurs. I'm listening with my ear flush against the door so I can make out something. She's just woken up, surprised. Then she gets shrill. She's arguing. She's angry. Now Terry Carbon's raising his voice. They both are loud enough for the rest up the band to come out of their bedrooms rubbing sleep from their eyes.

"What's going on?" Evan asks. His hair is standing on its end and he couldn't look cuter. I shrug one shoulder.

"Who's that with Clarissa?" Randy asks. "Bad hookup?"

"It's Terry Carbon," I whisper. "He just showed up."

Now we're all listening at the door. It's clear to everyone what's happening. We hear Clarissa screaming. Then stomping coming closer to the door. We all back up as she bursts out like a fetus being born. Her face drenched with tears; beet red. Terry Carbon is whistling behind her.

"He's cut me," she cries, giving Terry an accusatory finger.

None of us say anything.

"From the band," she continues, as if it's not clear.

"It's not working out," Terry says, and points to the ceiling. "This came from the higher-ups."

"I *started* this band," she says, thumping her chest. "Evan, *we* started this band. It's our idea."

"No, it was all of ours," Ed says. "We were at Café Hey and Evan has his guitar—"

"Oh, shut up, Ed," Clarissa thunders. "No one has ever cared what you think!"

"Now I don't think that's true," Ed says.

"You all are a bunch of morons," she says. "*I* was the one who got everyone serious. I was the one who got Lacey involved."

Now Lacey has woken up too. When Clarissa eyes her to verify, Lacey looks down at her bare feet.

"Really?" Clarissa shrieks. "No one is gonna come to my defense."

She turns to Evan. A mistake, since he's already focused on his own feet. Now she turns to me.

"You did this."

She's in my face, a screeching demon ready to tear into whatever's in her way. And then she's on me and we're rolling around on the floor. She's yanking my hair because she's a weak fighter. I get a punch in the face.

There's scuffling all around us and we're pulled apart. She spits out blood. I see a chunk of my blonde hair looking like a warped bird's nest on the floor.

"Get offa me, get offa me," Clarissa's raging. Ed's got her held tight.

"Sweetheart, have some dignity," Terry Carbon says, and winks at me.

"Oh, fuck you." Clarissa manages to wrestle out of Ed's grasp. She jumps at Evan, points at his chin. "You're a weak man. You all deserve each other."

And then she tears off out of the basement apartment and out of our lives, hopefully for good.

"Well, that was a spectacle," Terry Carbon says, brushing himself off because that's what you do after a tussle. "I think she completely justified why this had to be done. I'm gonna get a drink down the street."

Ed, Randy and Lacey follow him, all agreeing. Evan and I left in the hallway with a tuft of my ripped-out blonde hair between us.

"That was nuts," he says.

"Totally nuts. But she brought this upon herself."

I give another one shoulder shrug, my signature move for the day. Acting as if I know nothing. He's watching me closely. He's aware, even if he doesn't want to admit it. How I set this in motion. How I'm a creep aimed to destroy what gets in my way.

"Let's get that drink with them," I say, picking up the tuft of hair and tossing it in the trash.

18

• • • • •

Tomorrow – Silverchair

Recording the album in the studio is intense but such a dream. It's as if we've been exorcised after Clarissa got cut, the bad energy no longer messing with our mojo. We stay until late at night every night and my vocal cords are killing me, but I'll give it my all in every song from the opening track "Ready to Guide" to our closer "Big Toe". The execs seem happy with how the album is going, especially Terry Carbon who boasts to anyone in earshot how he "discovered us".

"They were raw, this mish-mosh band from Oregon, but I saw potential. I saw how Nico commanded an audience."

I could never get tired of hearing myself praised. We're spoken about as if the state of the record company depends on us. Nirvana's *MTV Unplugged* album is about to be released and the execs are sure it will be a huge hit. But what would happen after that with no more Nirvana? Kurt Cobain could never be replaced and it looks like Dave Grohl is gonna move on to another band, but there's no way it'll be as successful as Nirvana. The industry is fiending for whoever will take their place and we're being primed to fit into that groove. Gen X is getting older, they'll be starting families soon. They won't have the time to give their hopeless devotion to bands anymore. The grunge scene would still exist, but not hold the power it once did. We hear the word "poppier" thrown about. That the music industry would move away from an Alice in Chains heroin-y feel to a sound that's slightly more uplifting. While our songs deal with addiction and suicide, alienation and troubled teens, there's a hope in our lyrics as well, like with "Big Toe" for example. That's the sound of tomorrow.

Every day in the studio is a grueling one, beginning early in the morning and stretching until we're all so tired: Evan and Randy's fingers bleeding, Ed's hands full of calluses, my throat shot. I drink lemon and ginger and honey and do vocal exercises each morning at dawn to prepare. When we make it back to the apartment, we're too wiped to even speak to each other. We go to bed and hit the pillow so hard it hurts. Some of the band starts taking uppers, but I refuse. I'm afraid to try it once and have it ruin my groove. My routine is a flask in my pocket that I sip whenever I have a moment free. I'm bombed most of the time, but it doesn't affect my voice. I believe it makes it stronger. I really do. It eliminates my nerves. It gets me to zero in on one thing and that's the music. I've never felt it so strongly. Shot into my veins. Our sound drips with my blood. It's a living, breathing entity with us all. And just in case I forget the words, I have them scrawled all over my arms and hands for reference. I see them in my sleep. Each song a story I crawl through, bring to life. We do a song a day, over and over until we get it right. Sometimes a note is off, or Ed comes in too soon. We've even been too perfect, not raw enough. We need to find the balance. With "Ready to Guide" I'm forced to imagine Kristen again and again because the sound lacks oomph if I don't. I need to get myself to a state just before bawling and then we can begin. It's torture, but beautiful torture, because that's the kind of devotion it takes to make true art. All this sacrifice.

I haven't talked to Winter or Jeremy in forever, since I don't want to be pulled into Winter's inevitable drama with her guy. I want to call Jeremy, but it seems like all of a sudden I'm so far removed from them, and it's not as if either ever call to check in on me. We even have a song about that – "Friendshit", detailing what happens when old friendships begin to crumble. How you can't rely on people only because you have a history. As you get older, it's simply not enough.

As we near the end of the album, I realize I haven't been sober at all for over a week. My stomach is a mess and I've barely eaten because we have no time for food. I imagine I've lost weight, but I hear from Terry Carbon that a Kate Moss look is good, so I feel like I'm doing exactly what I'm supposed to.

If I think of Clarissa, it's only in a superior way, proof that I'm capable of getting what I want if I put my mind to it. She could be in a ditch now for all I care, and Evan has never brought her up since she left. He's aware of what I did and likely finds my drive hot, even though he could never admit it. Sometimes when we're recording, we'll eye fuck each other and I imagine us on a giant stage playing to the world. A single on the radio in everyone's car. A music video that hits number one on MTV's *Top 20 Countdown.* A tour where we get to see the world. In the moments when we have our eyes lock, I feel safe. Like whatever will happen in the future to Grenade Bouquets will be okay because we'll have each other to get through it. I hope he thinks the same. I'm tortured when he looks away, lost in his own guitar licks. When we finally record "Big Toe" it's just he and I in the booth, a quiet song, a love song, showcasing our relationship. And when I sing the last lyric I cry because this part of the journey is over. I'll never record my first album again. We'll never be so innocent. We'll be thrust into the limelight and like rabid dogs they'll feast on us. We'll be exalted and then what? How many bands truly last forever? I glance at all my band members. Randy drumming on his lap, Ed nodding to the beat, Lacey obsessively studying our every move, Evan playing a final chord and my closing note lasting for an eternity, holding my breath because I don't want it to end. And when it does, the room erupts into cheers, but I'm drunk and nervous about tomorrow: what it will bring, how it will change me, likely never to return to who I was.

I vomit onto my shirt, no bits of food, all booze. Everyone laughs because what else are you supposed to do? Calls for celebration are shouted out. Bottles of champagne are brought, the corks popping like gunshots. Tiny bubbles down my throat as I sip in my bra, the wet shirt tossed, cheersing with everyone, trying to ignore a voice deep down that's whispering "beware", "beware of tomorrow", and I think of Macbeth, the last book I read in school from what seems like another life.

"*Tomorrow, tomorrow, and tomorrow. The days creep slowly along to the end of time. And every day that's already happened has taken fools that much closer to their deaths.*"

Maybe I'm still too drunk, and I get super maudlin when I'm like that.

19

• • • • •

Interstate Love Song – Stone Temple Pilots

Grouch Records puts us on a multiple city tour down the coast to build buzz for the album: New York, New Jersey, Baltimore, D.C., Fort Lauderdale and Miami. Traveling in a bus is an upgrade from the VW and makes us think we're hot shit. We're always the opener, never the headliner yet, a total of five songs max. We close with "Ready to Guide" soon to be released on the radio. They're the biggest shows we've played yet, upwards of a hundred people in each venue. Our new publicist Liz Mesner, given to us by Grouch, explains how it's better to start small. Put a band like us with a giant one and we'll get drowned out. This way we're potentially being talked about over the headliner.

By Jersey, we already have a write-up in *Spin* magazine. It's no more than half of page but they use the picture of me after I knocked Clarissa into the mosh pit. We're called "The band about to blow up your world". We play our first show where some strange liquid isn't leaking from the ceiling and joke that "this is making it". Liz Mesner watches us like a trained bird of prey. She has a haircut with severe bangs, and I can spot her black bob anywhere. She seems to never smile, only speak out of the corner of her mouth, and wears power suits with tall high heels. She's my idol.

We start to fall into our roles. Evan and I up front on the stage. Randy in back on drums with Ed keeping the bass beat. When we're asked for autographs, it's usually for me and Evan. Stupid girls flock to him after a show. Skanks wearing as little as possible, putting on lip gloss in front of him so they have an excuse to make a kissy face. They glom on, using any excuse to touch him. He's shy and always polite while I want to tear off their heads. The girls who come up to me are the ones who hide their bodies under their baggy clothes. They dress dark and usually mumble that a friend of theirs heard about me. That I'm so dope. They want to know when our album is coming out. I tell them "soon" and give hugs. I sign notebooks, an arm, once a cast. I make an eye symbol over the "I" in Nico. I decide that'll be my signature.

We have a day off in Asbury Park and go to the beach, even though it's cold. There's a light snow along the sand, early for November. Ed flings his clothes off and goes skinny dipping. He emerges all shriveled and we laugh. I do cartwheels along the sand/snow, and when I kiss Evan our lips freeze together. I've never kissed him in the cold before, realizing that we've now been together almost six months, my longest relationship yet! We sleep on the bus, each of us getting a tiny bed stacked on top of one another. Evan's on the top bunk and in the middle of the night, I crawl up to him and we bone. I bite my lip, so I don't wake up everyone, picturing Liz Mesner frowning at our two-a.m. copulation. I manage not to shriek, even though Evan can certainly get me there. Afterwards, I'm nestled in his arms, his beard tickling my forehead. He's lightly snoring so I whisper, "I love you," out loud. I do and have wanted to say it for a while, but hadn't had the guts. He stops snoring and I eat my heart, waiting for him to respond, but then he keeps snoring. Saying it out loud is enough for now, even if he didn't hear.

In Baltimore we eat crabs, using tiny hammers and a bib before our show. I wear the bib that says Barry's Blue Crab Shack on stage like it's part of my ensemble. I thrash and moan, rip the bib off and toss it into the crowd where it gets mauled. Two girls fighting over a crab-crusted bib that *I* wore. Crazy. After the show, I sign it for one of them. We go out afterwards, and I'm freaking out a bit. There are actual groupies that have followed us to the bar. One is even trying to get with Ed. Another two are attempting to hook up with Randy and Evan but get turned down. I slip my arm around Evan so his groupie catches the hint. She sulks away. But it doesn't stop there. Another girl with fishnet stockings and T-Shirt under her dress is hella flirting so I start downing Alabama Slammers so I can be cool and funny and keep his attention. He's drinking too and soon the bar is closing. We're drunk and falling into each other outside. I tumble in the snow, skin my knee, and he kisses my boo boo. "I love you," I tell him for real this time, my teeth chattering because I'm wearing a thin velvet vintage coat like I'm still in L.A. His brow knots. I hiccup and wave it away like it's no big deal. "I love you too," he says, and he's slurring his words and maybe only said it because I did but I choose to believe it wholeheartedly. We're by the Patapsco River and I must be shivering so he takes off his coat and wraps it around my shoulders.

"We have groupies," he says, nuzzling my hair. I'm jazzed about that but I wanna keep talking more about how we love each other.

I don't want to push it, though. I wanna be cool so I nod and say, "You have more groupies than me."

"It's only little girls," he says, with a flick of his wrist. "They're young, they idolize."

I picture girls plastering posters of us up on their bedroom walls. Drawing hearts around Evan's face. Going to sleep with the glow of their nightlights outlining him so he submerges into their dreams. I imagine them hating me as much as I used to be jealous of Courtney Love before I grew up and began to appreciate her massive talent. We walk back to the bus with our hands in the backs of each other's jean pockets. We're too drunk to make love so just hold each other until a surge of puke creeps up my throat and I have to run to the bathroom. That's the third time this week I've vomited my dinner, if I even had anything to eat. I know that's not good but figure I'll chill out after this mini tour ends. The booze is necessary right now for my nerves and my psyche and because I wanna have a good time. I've worked hard to make this happen and am ready to enjoy some fruits of my labor.

In D.C. I go hard before the show. I'm swaying on stage but maintain. Once again it helps me tap into the flow of the notes so we're soaring together.

In the audience I spy Liz Mesner's bob 'do. Every time I start to lose balance, I use her severe bangs to guide me back. She's a buoy in a mosh pit and I'm holding on for dear life. After the set, she finds me at the bar, tugs on my dress.

"Party girl," is all she says.

"No," I reply, but the vodka shot in my hand says otherwise.

"We use it for a little kick, not as a crutch. We clear, Nico?"

I swallow a lump in my throat but not the shot.

"I'm sorry."

She wags her finger back and forth. "No, no, no. No sorry. You're the talent."

I place my hand over my heart. "I am."

"Pace yourself." She swipes the shot from me and does it herself like a pro without even wincing. "We still have Florida."

When we reach Florida, I peel off my heavy sweater psyched to be in the warmth again. I am an L.A. girl always and forever and used to the sun. In Fort Lauderdale, we tan and let the beach remove our hangovers from D.C. We're harmonizing "Interstate Love Song" by the Stone Temple Pilots and Lacey says she loves when we do an acoustic number. We decide to play that cover on stage. It's our biggest venue yet, the headliners this band Daisy Chain that are big down here. A little more of a grunge hippie vibe so there's girls without bras and braided hair with a flower behind their ear. The guys all have long, unwashed hair and the b.o. is ripe. They don't mosh but sway in unison, singing along to our cover of "Interstate

Love Song" because they don't know the words to our original tunes. They take out lighters and a sea of flames flicker before me. I'm choked up as they clap and cheer and call us out for an encore. I give them a stripped down "Ready to Guide" and there's a girl in the front, a little pixie with short, spiked blonde hair and a button nose, her face flushed with tears. She's reaching toward the stage and I reach back and take her hands. She squeals and can't contain herself, jumping up and down as tears fly from her eyes. When I finish the song, I bow and book it to the dressing room. I'm trying to catch my breath but it's hard. I have a tiny bottle left in my purse like you would get on an airplane. It's Bacardi rum and I suck it down.

I don't know why I got so overwhelmed.

The drink calms and I can breathe again. I pop a mint in my mouth and meet the band outside to watch Daisy Chain. It's hippie noodle music and someone's joint gets passed my way. I take a large toke and weave my hands to the ceiling. I don't give back the joint to whoever was so kind. I toke until my eyes sparkle. Evan finds me and we wrap our arms around each other through the set. When we leave it's humid and I want to strip off my clothes like Ed did on the beach in Asbury Park. I'm halfway through getting my shirt off when Evan stops me. "Don't do that," he says. He makes me keep it on, tells me it's time to go to bed.

"I want to protect you," he says.

I'm cold now because it's nighttime, and even in Florida, it cools. I regret trying to take off my shirt and be "that girl". I want to be good.

In Miami, we have a show at an outdoor venue. It's

on the beach and the crowd is building. I suck down a few Pina Coladas before our set. If Liz Mesner sees, she doesn't say anything. Lacey is on the stool next to me and takes my hands.

"I'm so proud of you, Nico."

"Of us," I say, and wipe the pineapple foam from my mouth.

"Single goes on radio next week."

I pinch myself. "It's hard to even believe."

The roar of the crowd reaches us, hungry for our show. There must be three hundred people in the audience, a sea of sweaty bodies. Guys with their shirts off and flannels tied around their waists. Girls in jeans shorts with the pockets frayed and black boots with belt buckles, a men's checkered shirt and big sunglasses, hair bleached blonde with the roots showing. A permanent scowl on all.

Lacey takes off her grandma glasses and rubs a tear from her eye.

"Lacey, what's wrong?"

She takes out her old lady purse and removes a Kleenex. "Promise you won't get too big for me."

I'm drunk but try to follow. "What are you talking about?"

"Like you're about to hit big time, and I'm just this small manager from Oregon. I can't compete."

I shake her shoulders and she's a little surprised. "Lacey, you're the reason we're here. You booked our early shows, you got us that write-up in Guitar Picks. You brought me into this band!"

"Liz Mesner won't even acknowledge me."

We see Liz Mesner coolly sipping from a tall glass

and eye judging everyone around her.

"Screw her. I promise we'll never turn on you. You are Grenade Bouquets."

I hold out my pinky for a pinky promise and we wrap our pinkies and kiss our thumbs. She wipes her tears away.

"I'm sorry, that was stupid of me." She tries to laugh it off. "You have your show to do. Don't let me bother."

"I love you," I say, and really mean it. I'm getting good at throwing those words around. And I really do love all these new people in my life, just like I loved Winter and Jeremy, maybe even more. My heart stings a drop at the thought of them. Wondering if Winter is enjoying her motorcycle extravaganza and if Jeremy made other friends at school without us there.

"Nico," I hear Evan say, and forget about my old friends altogether. He has his hand out and pulls me up on stage. The band tunes their instruments. The lights begin to flash. The ocean laps gently, the air full of salt. The crowd looking up expectantly. I am their shepherd through this night. I pull the mic stand closer, ground my feet so I don't sway.

"How are you, Miami?"

Miami gives a resounding cheer back.

"So, this is our last stop on our first official tour with Grouch Records."

Woo-hoo!

"And our first single 'Ready to Guide' is about to hit the motherfuckin' radio, y'all. How hella dope is that?????"

Yeahhhhhhhhhhh!

"We're known for being a rough and tumble bunch," I say, smirking. "We like to blow shit up."

Awwwww yeahhhhhh!

"Because we're Grenade Bouquets and we are DA BOMB!"

I mime an explosion and the crowd goes wild. The feedback from the amp buzzes and I hear Randy go, "Two, three, four," and then the crushing sound of his drums, Ed's steady bass, and Evan's cool licks, as I bring the mic to my lips and destroy.

20

• • • • •

In Bloom – Nirvana

I'm sure there's always moments in life you'll remember, like when you get married, or hold your newborn baby, but like, I can't imagine anything more hella cool than hearing your song on the radio for the first time. After our tour, Evan and I are joyriding in the VW. We want a break from the rest of the band. Grouch Records is planning another tour soon, and we'll all be sandwiched together on a smelly bus for weeks and weeks, so it'll be hard to find moments to be alone with Evan. We drive out of the city up to Hudson Valley and pass horse farms, the trees all turning yellow with leaves falling, a fine layer of snow on the ground. A bottle of Gordons sits between us and we share sips but he's driving so he sips less. I'm flipping through radio stations from KRock to Z100. Pearl Jam plays, some Toadies, Blind Melon. We sing along to "No Rain", he calls me a bee. And then, magic happens.

"We got a brand-new song from a band that's been getting a lot of buzz," the DJ says.

Evan and I eye each other, not wanting to go crazy yet for fear they're speaking of someone else.

"'Ready to Guide' from Grenade Bouquets," the DJ continues.

I nearly wet myself and scream so loud I scare Evan. But then he's punching the ceiling in delight with his other hand on the wheel as we roll down the windows and crank the music. My voice pours into Hudson Valley, this ode to Kristen, and I hope it's loud enough that she can hear it in heaven or wherever she's gone now. The hairs on my arm stand on end, in disbelief that it's actually my voice coming from the radio. People are in their cars or at home singing along to my song. It's surreal. I reach for the Gordons and take a feisty sip. Some spills down my chin and I laugh it away.

Evan's singing too and we belt out the song together. I pass him the Gordons but he declines, so I take more.

"Go easy," he says, during an instrumental section. But I don't listen. I want to celebrate. And nothing is better than being a little sloppy, sticking my head out of the window, and shouting the lyrics that I WROTE.

> *Your ghost remains inside*
> *Ready to Guide*

"Okay, okay, Nico," he says, pulling me back inside the van.

"Okay, dad," I say, rolling my eyes.

"That was the new song 'Ready to Guide' by the band Grenade Bouquets," the DJ says. "You're gonna be hearing a lot more from them I assume. Just make sure not to piss them off, the lead singer's known to throw a punch."

"That's me!" I toast myself and have another sip. Now I'm quite toasty, smiling so hard it begins to strain.

All of a sudden, everything gets spinny and I'm lightheaded. I hold onto the dashboard to maintain and a flash of when I almost crashed my car sends my anxiety reeling.

"Nico, are you okay?" Evan asks.

"Pull over."

"Nico…"

"Pull over!"

He drives onto the shoulder and comes to a stop. I fling open the door and flop out, tripping over my boot laces and crashing to the dirt. I puke up the Gordons and an unfortunate McRib with fries. Evan's rubbing the back of my head.

"I'm okay, I'm okay."

I try to stand but my knees go wobbly.

"You had too much to drink," he says, all stern.

"Thanks again, dad."

I wipe away the puke and do a curtsey, trying to be cute.

"Ya-know Liz Mesner said…" Evan begins.

"What? What did Liz Mesner *say*?"

"Just that…" He nibbles at his lip.

"Did she tell you to monitor me?"

He kicks a pebble. "Well, yeah."

"Ugh, so I drink. Big deal. Like, it's different when you perform as a singer. All eyes are on you, ya-know? It takes a lot of courage."

"Totally. Just, I've seen you puke a few times."

I cross my arms and start to walk away. "I'm not

like an alcoholic or anything."

"No one's saying you are."

"No, it's the way you're looking at me. Because of what happened after Cobain died and I took that pill from those weirdos."

"Nico, I'm not even thinking about that."

"Like I have my shit together. I'm not as gutted about my sister anymore. I've accepted it."

He goes to hug me. "Look, our single's on the radio. I don't wanna fight."

"I don't either!"

Now I'm crying and my mascara is running and I must look crazy.

"Come here." He folds me into his arms. I put my nose into his neck and inhale his Cool Water scent. "We have a single on the radio." He shakes me. "We have a *single* on the radio."

"I know, I know."

He's tickling me and I can't stay mad and then he's chasing me and when he catches up, he tackles me to the grass on the side of the road and we're making out.

"I taste like puke."

"I don't care."

"Just don't police me, okay? I can handle myself."

He raises two fingers. "Scout's honor."

"I heard my voice on the radio," I say, gushing.

"Yeah, you did. Sexy as hell."

When we get back in the car, the radio's playing "In Bloom" by Nirvana and I wonder how it was for them the first time they heard their song on the radio. It would have been "Love Buzz". I imagine Kurt would act too cool to care, like it was no big deal. He likely wouldn't have screamed out of the moving van and then barfed up his Mickey D's.

But which way is honestly more rock star?

We drive back to the city, singing "In Bloom". There's a few sips left of the Gordon's bottle so I take them and while Evan looks over, he doesn't say anything. He lets me be me. And that is why I love him. I cheers to us as the final drop spills down my gullet and then toss the bottle on the highway, delighted when I hear it crash.

21

• • • • •

Girl, You'll Be a Woman Soon – Urge Overkill

Before our first video shoot, the band sees "Pulp Fiction" in the theaters and we can't stop quoting it. Singing "Girl, You'll Be a Woman Soon", by Urge Overkill and calling each other "gimp". I'm asking Evan to make me "blueberry pancakes" in a baby voice, and we marvel about the resurrection of John Travolta's career and mimic the dance between him and Uma Thurman in the retro diner. It gives us enough of a rush to film our video, and I only had a few sips of rum from the flask I brought with me. Enough to be cool when we arrive at the shoot.

A stage has been set-up in a run-down warehouse. The director, Nels Harlicker (real name), is a Euro-dude with multiple scarfs and spikey hair. His "vision" is of the band playing on stage and slowly becoming more and more deranged while I encounter a ghost who shows me the light.

"Am I dying in it?" I ask.

He shakes his tiny head. "No, the ghost will guide

you on your path. We'll finish the shoot up in the woods tonight."

I'm rushed to hair and makeup where a slim man prods my unwashed 'do and makes a *harumph* sound.

"No good?"

He doesn't respond, simply gets to work. I'm sprayed with enough hair product to widen the hole in the ozone layer. For makeup, I'm given bitten-red lips with a wash of pink blush, spider lashes with lilac pastel lids and blue eyeshadow with speckles of glitter. At wardrobe, I'm tossed a navy-blue lace dress and I put a gash at the bottom that shows one thigh. I choose an opal choker and drippy smiley face earrings as if they were made by Dali along with alien midi rings for my fingers. I suck on a watermelon Jolly Rancher to coat my tongue red, and I'm ready to go.

The set-up is as if the band is on stage for a talent show. We're shy and wave to the crowd, begin our song as if we're mild-mannered musicians, and then we RAGE. I go berserk and try to eat the mic. Evan's on his back noodling his guitar. Randy's playing his skull instead of the drums. Ed's humping his bass. The crowd (they'll be filmed separately) throws lettuce and tomatoes at us (that gets filmed now). I pick up a head of lettuce and tear into it with my teeth. Evan's stomps the tomatoes until my dress is coated red. I stick out my tongue, throw up devil horns, rip my dress at the gash even more until the bottom comes off and it becomes a mini skirt. Nels is screaming, "More, more, give us more, leave it all on the stage," so I stomp over to Evan, pull him up from the floor, and madly kiss him, making sure to bite his lip so it draws blood. He winces but goes along with it and blood is dripping down our chins as we feast on one another. When he wrestles away from me it looks as if he made out with a vampire. I stick out my tongue as the director calls "cut!"

"Brilliant, brilliant," Nels says, clapping his hands. Liz Mesner whisks by and gives a cool nod too. Lacey runs over and gushes.

"Now we only need Nico for the rest of the shoot in the woods," Nels says.

"How come?" Ed asks, his voice sounding more confrontational than I would expect.

"It's her story," Nels says. "Her ghost, her path." He sweeps by me. "Nico, you have an hour to change and then we'll go."

He kisses me thrice on each cheek and then claps away, barking at his assistant for an espresso.

"It's *her* story," I hear Randy say, mimicking Nels.

"What?" I ask, rejoining them on the stage.

"We're like the fucking background," Ed says. "Don't you see that?"

"Ed…" I hear Evan say, dabbing his bloody lip with a tissue.

"The shoot was awesome," I say. "The video is gonna be amazing."

"But you're the centerpiece, Nico, don't you see?" Randy says, tossing his drumsticks.

"I mean…it's just the end. Like the main part of this video will be us on the stage."

"Don't fool yourself," Ed says. "This is how it's gonna be. You in the front, us chop liver."

"Dude," Evan says, stepping toward him. "It's not her fault."

"I'm not saying it's her fault," Ed says. "I'm only stating the reality."

Randy pipes up: "And the reality is Nico's the star. Did I get three kisses on my cheeks from the director? Nope. We weren't even given wardrobe. I'm wearing what I had on when we saw *Pulp Fiction*."

"Blueberry pancakes," I say, because I don't know what else to add.

"This solidified it," Ed says. "And look, I'm glad I know my role. All our roles. We're here to support you."

Lacey finally opens her mouth to back me up. "Guys, this is what happens. The lead singer gets the spotlight in the video. It's an all-guy band with a female fronting it like Garbage. Shirley Manson is the one pushed to the front."

"Why are we fighting now?" Evan asks. "This was our first video shoot. Like, it was awesome. I flopped around on my back and played guitar. My girl rocked it."

"You can say that because you're the only other one in the band that gets any notice," Randy says. "Like the two good looking ones and then us ugs in the back."

Randy points his drumstick at Ed. "Who you calling ug?"

"The bassist and the drummer, no one gives a shit about us," Ed says. "No one comes up to us for an autograph. Even in the *Spin* article we're barely mentioned."

"This is ridiculous," I say, because I have no time for Ed and Randy. I have to change and get ready for the second part of the shoot. "Should I tell the director not to film me in the woods? I don't understand what you two want."

Ed and Randy look at one another.

"We want you to acknowledge this," Ed says, and Randy nods. "That you're the star. Own up to it."

"Fine!" I'm gnashing my teeth. "I'm the star. I took this band to the next level. Is that what you wanna hear?"

"That's exactly what I fucking what to hear," Ed says, and walks off. Randy follows.

Lacey rubs my arm. "Let me talk to them."

"Why are they being like this?" I'm close to tears and pissed that the two of them are ruining such an excellent day.

"Ego. Fear. Who knows?" Lacey says. "They're stupid men. They have five brain cells. No offense, Evan."

"None taken."

She runs after them and Evan hugs me.

"Don't let them bother you," he says. "It's a little jealousy. It'll wear off."

"They like blamed me. I have no say in anything the director does."

"I know, Nico. Forget about it. They'll chill out. Let 'em rant."

"I need to…change," I say, weaseling out of his arms. He looks hurt. "I mean, the director said an hour. I don't want to keep him waiting."

His kisses me on the forehead. "You're gonna do great."

We kiss on the lips and I laugh a little because his blond beard has bits of dried blood in it. I go to the dressing area and I'm breathing heavy. Looking in the mirror, I can see I'm shaken. I find my purse and remove the flask with rum. There's enough left for a few good swallows.

A car waits to take me to the woods. I have no idea where we're going. It's dark when we reach it. A crew has already set-up the shot. I'm to emerge from a thicket of trees and encounter my ghost. It'll be an image of myself so I'm to play dual roles. My ghost is dressed in a tattered white wedding dress. We film the ghost scenes first, which include the ghost reaching out to myself and beckoning me down a dark path. For the other shots, I give my hand over to this ghost and we run through the woods. My dress gets torn the further I go and I get cut up and leave trails of my blood. It's almost midnight when we finish and I'm covered in fake blood. I'm toasting the moon with what's left on my flask as Nels comes on over.

"Baby," he says, in his weird accent. "You're gonna be a star."

"We're all gonna be stars," I say, pointing at all the blinking lights in the sky. Out in the woods, the universe is giving us a stellar show.

He shakes his tiny head that looks like an eraser on a pencil. "No, no, no. You are *the* star." He points to the North Star, the one blinking the brightest, then winks at me.

A chill rushes up my spine. It's December and I'm in a dress in the woods, my shoulders and décolletage bare, my skin red and raw. I take out my flask but there's nothing left.

"Here," Nels says, and passes over a bottle of whiskey. "For your beautiful shoot. You deserve it, doll. You are a woman now, not a little girl. You have been formed."

He winks again, but I realize it's only a tic in his eye. I twist off the cap as the whiskey pours down and I'm warm again, any problems with the band melting away.

"Is this how it's always gonna be?" I ask the full moon.

It pulses with a definitive answer of "Yes".

22

• • • • • •

Bullet with Butterfly Wings – Smashing Pumpkins

Our song is tearing up the radio charts, so much that Grouch Records books an immediate show at the legendary CBGB before our main tour will begin. We're the opening, opening band still, but BFD (Big Fuckin' Deal), this is the big time! CBGB is beautifully grimy with graffiti all over the walls, dank and brooding, the ceiling looking like it's about to collapse, the floor uneven and threatening a tetanus shot, cramped and dark, filled to capacity with older punks and long-haired dudes, girls in tanks despite the cold, safety pins in noses, makeup to look like ghosts.

I'm in the bathroom, a claustrophobic hellhole with graffiti written over other graffiti, a toilet that's seen better days. I'm puking but nothing's really coming up because I've barely eaten all day. This has become more and more the norm. It's like I don't have time anymore to shove food into my mouth and it's starting to show. My chipmunk cheeks have given way to ac-tual cheekbones. My waist no longer has girth and my thighs lost any remnants of cottage cheese. As I wipe the bile from my lips in the mirror, I barely recognize myself but in a good way. Like the Nico I used to be was a child left in L.A. and a new queen has emerged.

"Five minutes," I hear along with a knock on the door. I think it's Lacey. I take a final sip from my trusty flask but stuff it in my brassiere anyway. We've never played a show at a famous venue like CBGB, and I'm shitting in my boots. But I wet my face, slick back my blonde mane, and stomp outside like a pro.

"You okay?" Lacey asks, as we head to the stage. I don't even look to see if she's giving me concerned eyes. Like she's worried but too afraid to say anything.

Yesterday I heard our song on the radio right before Smashing Pumpkins' "Bullet with Butterfly Wings", and I can't fucking believe I'm even in the same breath as them. The DJ segued from us to them like we were meant to be a part of the same breath. I still can't wrap my mind around any of it.

The rest of the band is on stage. Evan gives me a cool smile. Ed and Randy barely glance up. They're still butt hurt after seeing the final music video where a good chunk of me in the woods monopolized the shots of the band at the talent show. But the video is awesome and about to premiere on MTV and then holy hell shit is about to get nuts. At least what Terry Carbon tells us. He wasn't on tour with us but comes to this show wearing his signature sunglasses. I nod his way and he crosses his arms like, "Show me what you got, kid." Next to him stands Liz Mesner sipping from a drink, and before I can even attempt to wave, the lights go hot and the band starts up.

"We are Grenade Bouquets," Evan says into the mic, tossing his long bangs out of his eyes. He hasn't gotten a haircut since we first got to New York and I can never see his eyes anymore. He's shaggy and sexy and I want to bone him right there in front of the audience. The only part of the talent show that made the video was us kissing with blood dripping from our chins. "And you may have heard of us on the radio," he continues.

"Fuck yeah," I hear someone shout. A dude with a mohawk who raises his fist to the ceiling. The mosh pit ramps up and the crowd rolls around like a tornado. Boots scuffing, beer spilling, groans and chants. I launch into the glorious "Hole in a Bucket" with its dueling guitars, before wallowing in "Split" with its sad chorus, and then the hurt wails of "See-Saw". The crowd and CBGB becomes a part of the show. We're melding into one organism that exists only in the pursuit of a music high. I take out the flask from my bra and swig the alcohol around like its mouthwash before swallowing. The lights spiral, a dead thump from Ed's bass knifes the air along with the rat-tat-tat of Randy's drums and then Evan's shattering guitar for the opening chords of "Sunny Side Down". I'm a dervish on stage, whirling around, twisting the mic around my body. I'm singing so loud I can feel my uvula rattle. I'm scratching down my arms until blood blisters surface. I kick at a beer bottle rolling my way and it gets launched into the din of the crowd. They're so loud I don't even hear it crash. I take them through the brutal chorus before releasing them with its quiet final lyrics. We spiral back down to Earth, and they're all left stunned, thwacking into one another like zombies.

"Thank you, New York!" I yell. "I love this fucking city. This dirty and perfect paradise. I love the rats in the subways who nibble my toes. I love the meat on the stick from the vendors on the corners. And hot slices of pizza sticking to the roof of my mouth. And all these lives crashing together, but somehow it works. Your sirens and horns, your skyscrapers and trees up every block. Your cabs that cut me off and your amazing fuckin' music lovers that flock to all the venues here. Thank you for coming out tonight."

"Play 'Ready to Guide'," I hear a girl cry out. I spot her, teeth bared, drink in her fist. I leave my body and watch from above. No one's ever shouted a request before. This is unchartered territory.

"You want 'Ready to Guide'?" I scream back at them.

"Yeahhhhhhhhhhhh!"

"You got 'Ready to Guide'." I eye the rest of the band. "One, two, three, four."

I start singing but then something happens which nearly makes me take flight. The crowd is singing along. THEY KNOW THE FUCKIN' WORDS! I'm gushing in disbelief. And when I reach the chorus, they're singing louder than me.

Your ghost remains inside
Ready to Guide

Tears spill down my cheeks and I think of Kristen and how this song began. How I would never be here if not for her. And how sometimes tragedies can lead to bliss. I'm crying for the fans, for the song, and for her. She floats down from above, her ghost tapping to the beat, dancing around more uninhabited than ever before. She's a new Kristen. She's changed just like I have. We are fresh beings. And I love her so, so much.

"This is for you, Kristen," I say, once the song ends. I feel like a bullet with butterfly wings, someone who's gone through such hardship but finally taken flight. The crowd is cheering so loud I can't even think. They're screaming for more. I raise my hands to calm them down. Once they do, I begin singing an acoustic version of "Bullet with Butterfly Wings". Evan joins with quiet flicks of the guitar. Ed finds his way into the song as well along with Randy keeping a steady beat. We are unified again. We will rage against each other many, many times because that is what great bands are bound to do, but we are a family, and this is a moment of celebration. One we will never forget. The crowd is silent as I slow down the song, belt it from my heart. Kristen's ghost waves goodbye with a kiss. She comes now only when she feels like it, no longer a requirement, just a way to reunite and check in on one another, like living sisters would do.

The song ends and I give a bow.

"I'm Nico and we're Grenade Bouquets," I say, fully at peace for probably the first time in my life. "Thanks for letting us into your world."

23

• • • • •

Misery – Soul Asylum

It's late but since it's three hours earlier in L.A., I call Mom. I imagine her sitting down with a pot of tea and her boyfriend as they'd watch *Roman Holiday* and gush about how much they're in love. I can't wait to tell her about our show at CBGB, even though she'd have no idea what that is, and about having a single on the radio. I've gotten bad about checking in lately. If her or Dad left messages on the answering machine at the apartment, I haven't checked those in a month.

"Mom!" I yell, once she picks up. I'm outside at a pay phone and it's cold and snowing. Two homeless men are arguing over a Blimpie sandwich. "Mom, it's me," I continue, a little drunk but hopefully not noticeably too drunk. At least it'd been a minute since my last sip on stage.

"Nico..."

"So, we just played a show at CBGB!" I'm dancing in place. "It was like, so hella awesome. I mean, I can't even put it into words, Mom. You don't understand,

CBGB is like this *legend*ary place. I mean, The Ramones played there, you know The Ramones?"

"Yes, Nico, I know The Ramones."

"*I Wanna Be Sedated*," I sing. "Anyway, the crowd was packed and get this, they knew our song. Like, the one on the radio! Did I even tell you we have a song on the radio now? And we filmed a music video that's gonna be on MTV."

"Nico, that's very exciting," she says, calm as ever. I wanna yell, "Where's your fire, Lady?"

"It is exciting!"

The two homeless guys start getting physical over the sandwich and I turn my back to them.

"Thank you...and Dad. I mean, you both are letting me live out this dream and I'm sorry for any hell I put you through. Like, I was a demon, I can honestly say that. And, I'm...well, you know, just sorry if I was a shit to you."

"Thank you, Nico." She exhales a huge sigh that ices my ear. "Nico..."

"Uh-oh, what is it? That sigh isn't good."

"I left a message on your answering machine—"

"Yeah, we haven't checked that in days. Between the video shoot and prepping for—"

"Nico, Edina contacted me... It's about Winter. She..."

"What? She what?"

"Honey, Winter tried to kill herself."

My body goes cold. I drop the phone and scramble to pick it back up. I can barely speak.

"What? Is she okay? I mean, what happened?"

"She is okay," Mom says, firmly. "She's in a facility.

Edina put her in a facility."

"She was on a motorcycle trip," I say. I look up at the night sky and the swirling snowflakes make me dizzy.

"I don't know the details."

"She met this guy. He was older. They were gonna bike up the PCH together."

Snot is dripping from my nose, and I wipe it away only for more to pour out.

"I don't understand," I say, and I'm crying now. Angry at Winter and at myself for not being a better friend and checking in. "We haven't really been getting along. I don't know. I mean, I've been so busy. I haven't really thought about her."

"Nico, it's not—"

"And she must've been miserable. Like, it was all an act. This older dude. And her plan. I feel so shitty."

"Nico," Mom snaps. "This is not your fault. That girl… I've always thought she had issues. She's… no I don't want to assume anything. But this could not have been out of nowhere."

"Is she in L.A.?"

"Yes, a place here."

"I'm coming home," I say, not even giving it a second thought. Winter's my soul sister. We've shared our blood. We've been best friends since we were eleven. Our lives are entwined, or at least they used to be. She used to be the most important person in my life.

A robotic voice comes on the line and asks to insert more money to continue the call.

"Oh, fuck you," I say, digging around my pockets and finding a few quarters. I shove them in.

"Nico, you don't have to come home. You have your own life to lead."

"No, Mom. I can't be here now. Without knowing. Without being there for her. Like she's in some place all alone and she must be so scared. I'm gonna book a flight."

"Sweetie, she might not even want company right now."

"I don't care. She needs me. She… I'm gonna go right now. Like, the record company has given us petty cash. It'd be enough to fly home. I'll find an overnight flight. I'll be in L.A. by morning."

"I know I can't dissuade you. You're going to do what you want to, like you always do. If you need to be there for her…"

"*She* needs me to be there for her."

"All right then, honey. She's being monitored and not in any danger to herself, so just calm down. Do you know how to book a flight? You've never flown by yourself before."

"I know, I'll figure it out. It's no big deal, Mom."

"You've just…" Her sigh takes eons to finish. "You had to grow up so fast. I think back to being your age, and I was so sheltered. And what you've had to deal with."

"Mom, my quarters are gonna run out. Like, I need to go."

"You're strong. You're so strong. And I'm proud. Of you. Of everything."

I wipe my sleeve across my eyes. "Thank you."

"All right, honey. I'm sorry I had to tell you this."

"It's okay. I love you, Mom."

"I love you too. Take care."

I hang up the phone and the two homeless guys are still fighting over the sandwich.

"My best friend tried to kill herself," I scream at them, as I eat my tears. They look at me stunned.

"I'm sorry, girl," one of them says.

"I'm sorry too," I say.

A car shoots by playing Soul Asylum's "Misery". The song pumping from the windows, the driver crooning along.

The homeless men shuffle over, forgetting about the sandwich in the snow. One of them spreads his arms out. I fold into them, nestled by this strange embrace. He squeezes me tight, smelling of cat piss, but I'm not letting go.

I'm not ready to face this new reality.

A life, possibly, without Winter.

SIDE B
• • • • •
1995

24

• • • •

Pretend We're Dead – L7

The band understands I have to leave. We have a second of downtime anyway before our next tour and the video comes out and we'll need to do press. Flying back to L.A. is weird. It's hot for one and I've never spent a winter away so I'm overdressed. Mom picks me up and drives me straight to the facility in Topanga Canyon, a hippy-dippy place Edina must've found with wind chimes at the entrance. Mom and I don't speak much on the car ride over. I'm wiped from the overnight flight and try to catch a few winks. When we get there, she gives me a hug and tells me she'll be back soon to pick me up. As she drives away, I want to run and go with her, avoid dealing with visiting Winter in this state. But I put on my big girl pants and walk inside.

Jeremy's in the waiting area. He's dyed his hair blond, the tips black with a middle part. In his oversized baggy jeans and Marvin Martian T-Shirt, he looks so young. The life has been sucked out of his face, a ghoul stares back.

"It's been a rough few days," he says, after we hug.

"Is she okay?"

"She's…Winter. They like kinda sedate her."

"When will she be able to leave?"

He shrugs his shoulders.

"What happened?"

He brushes the hair from his eyes, a nervous tic. "I don't know everything. She went on that motorcycle trip with Don. He's an asshole." He rolls his eyes. "He'd call me queer all the time and trip me. A bad dude. But Emily's seeing his friend and they were like this foursome. She's different."

"Who? Winter?"

He nods. "I wasn't happy she was going anywhere with him, but like what could I say? She wouldn't have listened. Anyway, the gist was that she caught Don with Emily one night in a dump of a hotel they were all staying at and then she…" He sniffs back his tears. "She swallowed a bunch a pills."

I cover my mouth with my palm, shaking my head. "Oh, Jesus."

"They had to pump her stomach. I mean, it seemed like it was touch and go for a sec. But she's been stable since. They monitor her like crazy here, and Edina's been staying in her room."

"How's Edina?"

"She puts on a brave face, but I know this shook her. Winter's always dealt with depression—"

"I know, I know—"

"I think Edina always worried about this happening."

"Can I see her?" I ask, sounding like a child.

"Yeah, Edina's with her now." He glances at the

Teddy Bear in my hands. "Is that Benny Bear?"

"I had my mom bring me him. I thought she could use a friend."

Benny Bear's missing an eye and lost some of his stuffing, but he was my childhood bear and he and Winter used to always have a special relationship when she'd stay over for sleepovers.

"That's sweet, Nico. How are you?"

"I'm good, but I don't wanna talk about myself right now."

"No, girl, I wanna hear. Like I heard your song on the radio. Oh my God, Nico, I wet my pants. I mean, I didn't, but you know?"

"Yeah, things have been really good. I mean, with that."

"We can all use some good news right now." He rubs my arm. "I'm so proud of you, Nicorette."

I take his face in my hands and kiss him on the cheek. "I love you, Jer Jer."

He wipes away tears and we hug each other hard again.

"I'll be waiting here," he says.

Taking a deep breath, I steel myself for Winter. A guard has to frisk me and check my purse. He says nothing can be brought in that might be a weapon so I leave my purse with him. The place smells of antiseptic. Down a white hallway, nurses wander in and out of rooms. I'm wearing a belly-baring shirt and I'm nervous I look like I tried too hard, like I'm showing off. But I really just grabbed a bunch of clothes and threw them in a suitcase without much thought.

When I enter, Edina's by the door, her poof of orange hair pulled back with a giant clip. She's wearing a pashmina and looks as if she's lost weight. The bones in her neck and chest protrude.

"Nico," she whispers, and we embrace. I haven't looked over to Winter yet. I'm not ready to see, so I stay in that hug with Edina for a while. "I'm so glad you're here."

It seems as if she hasn't slept in days. The bags under her eyes have more bags.

"Ma, who is it?" I hear.

Peering over Edina's shoulder, Winter tosses in her bed. I see that she's strapped in and my stomach roils. I gotta hurl but hold it in.

"Baby, Nico's come to see you."

She presents me as if I'm a trophy. Winter seems less than thrilled.

"She's on some calmers," Edina whispers in my ear, and I nod. "I'm gonna leave you girls alone." She turns to me. "Happy, happy thoughts," she says, using her fingers to fix her smile. "That's best."

"Okay."

When she leaves, my heart drops. The AC in the room feels cold and my arms are covered in goose-bumps. I walk as slow as possible over to Winter's bed, each step a lifetime. I don't know what to say.

"Fuck," Winter says. "Are you gonna be like all the rest of them?"

I'm crossing my arms, my body turned in on itself. "How's that?"

"Like I'm nuclear."

Her face looks washed out. Without makeup she has barely any eyebrows or eyelashes, alien-like. She's in a light blue gown, her teeth gummy.

"Shut the door," she says, waving.

"Are you allowed…?"

"Nico, shut the fucking door."

"Okay." I slouch toward the door and shut it quietly.

"I'd kill for a cigarette," she says. "You don't have any on you?"

"They kept my purse."

"Nazis," she says, and then raises her voice. "That's what they are, Nazis."

I glance at the door, as if nurses are about to rush in, or maybe I just want to escape.

"Looks like you're stuck with me," she says, laughing. Winter was always good at reading my mind.

"Are you okay?" I finally ask. I'm beside her bed now. I want to hold her hand that looks so pale it matches the white sheets.

"Of course I'm okay." She gives a *harumph* like a bucking horse. "I mean, everyone swallows pills at least once in their life. I wasn't really gonna harm myself. I was just in the moment."

I think back to after Kurt Cobain died and I still hadn't gotten over Kristen's death. I wanted to drive my car into a lamppost and achieve lights out for good.

"I get it, Winter."

Her eyes sparkle. Her fang teeth show as she smiles, but it's a devilish one.

"Do you get it, Nico? Famous Nico."

"I'm not—"

"Should I bow down and kiss your dumb toes? Oh, thank you so much for rushing back to check on little old me."

"Winter, you scared me."

"Scared you? That's rich. Like you give a flying fuck. You're singing away and I'm not a thought."

"That's not true. I've worried about you—"

I bite my tongue.

"Worry? You don't have to worry about me, all right? Winter is always gonna be fine. This is a speed bump. Like I'm over it already."

"What happened?"

"I'm sure Jeremy told you everything."

"Just...a little."

"Don's a dick, okay? We're biking up the coast and the whole time he's with Emily too. Like he couldn't even have a fantasy of being with her and I at the same time like a normal dude. He's into mind games and shit. He wanted me to find out."

"Why?"

"I dunno. He's got issues, but for like two seconds, it was so hella fun. I mean, he's a bad boy, Nico. He sells drugs, he roughs me up a little."

"Winter!"

"Oh, climb down off that high horse of yours. Like your man is any better. Wasn't he messing around with his ex?"

"No, she's out of the band. And he'd never rough me up. God, Winter, what would he do?"

I'm so disgusted I'm practically shivering.

"Slap me around, nothing too serious. He's a biker dude, that's what they do. And I was his old lady. It was hot. Being on the back of his hog, no worries in the world. Like it was so freeing. I never felt so alive."

"I'm sorry."

"You don't have to be sorry. I know you love feeling sorry for me."

"That's not true."

"It's always been true." She cuts me with her eyes. "Your existence was based off the fact that I'm a bigger mess and always would be. As horrible as things might be for you, it's a guarantee that they're worse for me."

I squeeze my fists. "In case you haven't forgotten, I've had a rough ass year, Winter. Kristen fucking died—"

"Yes, I know this. We *all* know this, Nico. You went through a tragedy and therefore get to use it..." She tugs on her lip.

"Use it? What do you mean?"

"Pity. For everyone to feel bad. To stroke your cheek."

"I've never asked for any of that. And for you to say..." I calm myself, *woosah* like Aunt Carly would want me to do. *She's lashing out,* I tell myself. *That's all this is. She wants me to feel worse off than she does. Let her.*

"I don't want to fight with you," I say, exhausted. "I just want you be okay."

"When will you get it, Nico?" Silence spears the air between us. "I'll never be okay. It's just a question of when."

"When what?"

"When too many pills will be enough."

I tip my head back to the popcorn ceiling. I can't look at her right now. I don't know if she's serious or still trying to make me feel worse. I don't even know if I know who she is anymore.

"Winter, don't say that."

"It's my reality. So, go and sing your heart out on MT-fuckin'-V. And don't worry your pretty little face over me."

"You're my best friend, I'll always—"

"Well, stop," she shouts, and I stand rigid. I want to burst into tears but I hold them inside. I can't let her see me affected. "You're better off without me."

"Winter, c'mon."

She reaches up, maybe to fix her hair but she's tied to the bed and can't. She must've have forgotten for a second.

"This is a joke," she says. "Such a joke."

"I want to stay and be here for you."

"No, you don't. You have your eye on the exit. Like everyone in my life."

She twists her body so her head's facing the window.

"You can leave, Nico."

"I wanted to give you—"

"You can *leave*, Nico."

I'm stuck in place, not knowing what to do. Leaving Benny Bear on her bed, I head out of the room, only crying once I'm in the hallway, big globs of tears. Jeremy and Edina are there to comfort me.

"Oh sweet," Edina says. "She doesn't mean what she says. She loves you. She's so happy you came."

I nod but know that's not true. Edina is delusional about the way Winter feels about me. Just like she was delusional not to see the signs of Winter's decay.

My mom's car has pulled up to the lot. I say I have to go and burst outside.

"So soon…?" Mom asks, but then gets quiet because

she understands. It did not go well.

And I likely would never be coming back.

I don't want to talk on the ride home to Laurel Canyon. I have my mixtape in my Sony Walkman so I press play and L7's "Pretend We're Dead" assaults my eardrums, soothing me with its rotten and shimmering assault.

25

• • • • •

Ode to My Family – The Cranberries

I'm flying back to New York in the morning, but Mom and Dad want to get together at a restaurant with their significant others and even Aunt Carly drives down from Ojai. The last thing I want to do after leaving the facility is shove food in my mouth, but I haven't seen my parents since the trip started and I always miss Aunt Carly. Let's be honest, Aunt Carly is the main reason I'm going.

Mom drops me at home first where I shower. Afterwards, I'm lying in bed in a towel looking around my room and thinking that I don't even know the girl who used to live here anymore. She seems so far away from who I am now. A collage over the walls of cutouts from *Sassy* and *Jane* magazines. Trends I liked at one point. I remember when big hats with sunflowers were in. The few posters of Kurt Cobain I left up. A small TV with a VCR and a few of the same tapes I would watch over and over: *My Own Private Idaho* for River Phoenix of course and *Bram Stoker's Dracula* where I would rewatch the scene where Lucy would get plowed by the Dracula wolf, a Freddy Kruger toy, old Charm bracelets scattered across my desk from when I was a kid, a lavender Lava lamp, a fan that's older than me, enough candles to light the 1800s with all of them dripping down to the nub, Polaroids of me, Jeremy, and Winter through the years. I take one down of Winter bombed where she's sticking out her tongue and giving devil horns.

"Nico, you ready?" I hear Mom call out. "Reservation is for five-thirty."

I hate this California thing where everyone eats so goddamn early. In New York, I sometimes have dinner at nine or ten, if I even eat at all.

I dress and fold the picture of Winter into my pocket.

My parents pick this steakhouse they like that has giant booths so the five of us can fit. Dad is there in a suit with Annette. I guess he came from work. Roger Ferguson is picking at a gap in his teeth and then goes to shake my hand with the same one he was using to pick his food. F-ing gross.

"Where's Carly?" I ask, as we sit down.

"Is Carly ever early?" Dad asks. "She was born late."

"Peter," Annette coos.

"No really, she was born late."

The waiter brings waters and I'm thirsty as hell, so I gulp it down like I'm stuck on a desert.

"So, we heard your song on the radio, Scrap," Dad says, while tucking a napkin into his collar.

I don't want to talk about my song or anything else. I want to vent about Winter, but I don't know what to fucking say.

"Why so glum?" he asks, and then a second later realizes. "Oh, yeah. She's gonna be OK." He pats my hand twice.

"Why, because you say she is?"

His hand moves quickly to hold Annette's. "You kids, you think your problems are the world. But they aren't. It's teenage angst. It burns out."

Roger points to him in agreement. "I had long hair," he says, as if that explains everything.

"Rebellion. You're searching for a way to rebel."

"Peter," Mom says, in that voice.

"Not *her*, I mean, her friend…"

"Winter," I remind him.

"Yes, I know the girl's name. She was only over at our house every other night."

I'm about to put my head in my hands and call it a night when Carly waltzes in wearing a giant shawl and huge sunglasses like she's hiding from paparazzi.

"Sorry I'm late," she says, air kissing the table. "Nico…" She puts her hand on her hip. "My, my, my." She cups my chin. "Just fetching. Beautiful. Isn't she beautiful?"

She sits across from me, relegating Roger Ferguson to the end of the booth.

"How are you, child?" she asks, probing into my soul. My chin starts to tremble like Claire Danes's does when she cries.

"I'm…"

"Say no more," she says, waving her hands. "We don't have to discuss it."

It's weird because in some ways I need to talk about Winter, but I also want to forget her too. It was like that when Kristen died.

The waiter comes over and takes our order. Steaks all around with sides. The adults order a bottle of red and I get a White Russian. No one says anything. When it arrives, I suck it down hard and immediately my shoulders get slack and I'm swimming in its creamy vodkaness.

"So, the tour?" Carly asks, her teeth stained wine-red.

"Yeah, it was... It was amazing. I mean, we were up and down the coast and, like, people wanted my autograph and we shot a video and the song is doing really well on radio. Like, the fact it's even *on* radio."

"What was it like?" Carly asks. "To hear yourself?"

"Surreal. I left my body and was looking down from above."

"Mmm hmmm, mmm hmm," Carly says, fingering the crystal around her neck.

"We have press for the video coming up with MTV. It's all happening."

"Nico, we're so proud of you," Mom says. "And it's so good to see you. Well, not under the circumstances. You know? But, just to see you."

I cut into a fatty rib-eye. "It's nice to be home."

"Don't forget us little people," Roger Ferguson says, patting his rotund stomach. No one says anything.

"Nico," Carly finally says. "Do you have to use the ladies' room?"

"I..."

"Come, come," she says. "I'm just gonna steal her for a sec."

She whisks me out of my seat and Mom and Dad are left gaping as we power-walk down the hallway toward the bathroom. Inside, Carly locks it behind her. She throws her heavy purse on the sink.

"I could see you needed to get out of there," she says, digging through her purse.

"Yeah, they're, like, a lot."

Her eyes roll. "Tell me about it. Your father only looks at me with daggers." She digs some more and then gets an *aha* look. "Found it."

She pulls out a crystal that's kinda in the shape of a penis and hands it over.

"Hold it tight."

"Carly."

She closes her fist around mine, the penis crystal trapped in my palm sweat.

"Close your eyes. Breathe. Breathe out."

I do so a few times, feeling the crystal almost pulsating in my fist.

"Now open."

I am more relaxed once I do.

"Keep it," she tells me, and then hops up on the sink and lights a cigarette.

"I don't think you can smoke cigarettes in here."

She paws at her wild hair. "Oh, it's not a cigarette." She puffs. "Now, Nico, be real with me. Share your emotions." She reaches over a heavily-ringed hand and takes mine. "I know how much you love Winter."

"I'm mad at her."

"Why?"

"I dunno. She's like doing this for attention. She needs the spotlight."

Puff, puff. "It's deeper than that, baby. Depression is...well, she's one gnarly beast. Sneaks up on ya."

"You've had depression?"

"Always. You can't blame Winter."

"No, I don't. But I don't know what she wants from me."

Carly shakes her head. "Don't let her keep you here."

"I'm not, I'm flying home tomorrow."

"I mean mentally. You have a lot in your future to look forward to. Don't let her drag you down."

"But I don't wanna, like, not be there for her."

She passes me the finely-rolled joint. Probably the most perfect thing I've ever seen. I take a puff and it's strong stuff. Coughing, I pass it back.

"Jesus, Carly."

"Oh, this is from the gods. But listen to your wise aunt. There's only so much you can do for someone like Winter. I've met her. I know her. She'll always have crises. Some people need that to exist. You go spread your wings, and she'll be here when you get back. Or she won't. And then it wasn't meant to be."

I'm picking at a scab on my arm. I don't know how it got there. It's hard to imagine not having Winter in my life. Someone to turn to when every little thing happens. I always pictured us in an old age home together racing down the hallways in our super-powered robotic wheelchairs.

"She's watching you excel," Carly says. "And that can be hard. Look at you, you're stunning, Nico. You're a woman now. I can absolutely see that. If your parents can't yet and treat you like a child, don't worry about them. It's harder for them not to be biased. But I can. You've emerged from your cocoon. And I want you to soak up everything you're about to encounter."

She takes my face in her hands, the joint weaving its smoke into my hair.

"Blossom, child. And don't look back."

"OK, I promise."

"If you ever need me, you can call at any hour. You're the daughter I never had, always think of you that way. And if you need sanctuary, my home is a refuge. It's your home."

"Thank you, Carly."

We hug and I'm snotting on her shawl.

"And when you play California, you better be damn certain I'm gonna be the front row swaying my hips. My little Stevie Nicks. My beautiful Gypsy."

We hear a knock on the door and laugh and put out the joint. After taking a second to get our shit together, we march back out to face the world. "Ode to My Family" by the Cranberries is softly playing from speakers, and I'm so thankful for what I have, for my immediate family as crazy as they are, and for someone like Carly, who I think of like another mom as well.

We're holding hands as we get back to the table. Dad sniffs audibly but doesn't say anything. I slip the crystal into my pocket for when I might need it later. A little piece of Carly to carry with me at all times, even if it looks like an opaque penis.

26

• • • • •

Cornflake Girl – Tori Amos

I'm wiped when I get back to NYC. After taking a cab from JFK, I get home around midnight. No one seems to be around, the band probably out partying. I search for a note that Evan may have left but there's none. We talked right before my plane boarded and I told him I was coming back around midnight, so I assume he'll be home soon. He was kind on the phone and knows what I've been through with Winter. All I wanna do is cuddle with him and a bottle of wine tonight. Since he's not here yet, I find half of bottle of red that's the only thing sitting in the fridge and get to work.

I'm going over the trip and take out Carly's crystal penis. She's right that I can't let Winter affect me. Too much is at stake these next few weeks to have Winter gum it up. I can check in with Jeremy about her progress at the facility, or maybe it would be better if I didn't check up at all. Wait a month till things maybe calm down and then…

I hear giggling coming from down the hall. Grabbing

the bottle of red, I investigate. It's a lady's giggle coming from Lacey's room. A different lady's giggle follows along with Tori Amos's "Cornflake Girl" crooning from the doorjamb. Good for Lacey for finally getting some action. I know it's been rough for her to meet girls.

Just as I'm about to double back down the hallway and give them privacy, the door opens and Clarissa wanders out wearing only an XL T-Shirt that says Too Legit To Quit. She freezes in place, gives me a wicked smile before Lacey runs out in her own oversized T-Shirt and Scrunchie socks.

"Uh, Nico," Lacey says, with her deer in headlights gaze. "What are you doing here?"

I nearly drop the bottle of wine but recover.

"I just got back."

"Right." Lacey slaps her forehead. "I thought you were flying tomorrow."

"What does it matter?" I ask, as Clarissa giggles.

"It's good to see you." Lacey goes to hug me, but I step aside.

"What is *she* doing here?"

Clarissa scoops her arm around Lacey. "*She* is a guest of Lacey's."

"Are you fucking kidding me?"

I'm turning around and running down the hallway when I feel Lacey grab my arm.

"Nico, listen…"

I whip around. "She is poison. Don't you get it?"

Lacey looks small and hurt. Clarissa catches up and I can see them as a unified front—Clarissa's way of getting her hooks back in us.

Lacey fixes her grandma glasses that have sloped

down her nose. "Look, we were out the other night and Clarissa was there. And we got to talking. She apologized to all of us for everything. Like we're…"

"Cool now," they both say at the same time and then giggle some more.

"I'm sorry, Nico," Lacey says. "We just smoked a mega blunt. I'm really high."

"There's like a million girls in the city," I say, pointing the bottle of wine at Clarissa. "And are you even a lesbian?"

Clarissa taps her chin. "I don't believe in labels. I believe in love."

"Oh, sweetie," Lacey says, pursing her lips.

I'm about to barf. "Sweetie? You guys are a full-on couple?"

They turn to each other and giggle again.

"Stop giggling!"

"It's really good weed, Nico," Lacey says. "This won't affect the band. And like, I deserve to be happy too, right?"

I take a swig, the red wine hot down my throat. "Of course. I mean, yeah you should be happy. But she's evil."

"Ouch, Nico, tell me how you really feel," Clarissa says. "Look, I always had a thing for Lacey. She's awesome. So, we don't need your approval."

I chug more, wipe the wine residue from my mouth. "I know. Of course, I know that."

Clarissa steps toward me and takes the bottle of wine from my hands before swigging as well. "I'm not here to mess with you either. I'm over the band. Really. I'm working at Unique in the East Village. It's a clothing store. It's where I got this tee. I got a place on Bowery with these girls, and I'm working on my own music too. Like a retro Samantha Fox vibe. You know, 'I Wanna Have Some Fun'. Like, I'm over moody shit and Grenade Bouquets too. Nothing against you guys, though, it seems like things are amazing."

I grab back the bottle but there's only swill left. "They are."

"Great," she says, but I can tell she doesn't mean it. This is all some act by her to seduce Lacey and get in my head. And poor Lacey is too naïve to even see it.

We hear footsteps coming to the front door and the band bursts in wasted. Ed is carrying Randy on his back, who looks dead. Evan stumbles in after them. All stop cold when they run into our powwow in the hallway.

"How was Max Fish?" Clarissa asks.

Ed lowers Randy, who can barely stand up straight. "It was good. Hey, Nico."

I give an unenthused wave. "Hi."

"Hey," Evan says, coming over and scooping me up. "Did you just get back? How was your flight?" His breath smells of so much beer.

"It was a flight."

He kisses my neck. "I missed you."

"Were you gonna tell me about her?" I whisper into his ear and wriggle out of his arms.

"I felt like you were dealing with so much."

He gives me puppy dog eyes but I'm ignoring.

"Yeah, how's your friend?" Ed asks.

"Right," Lacey says, jumping in and trying to earn brownie points. "How is she?"

"Um, she hates my guts and probably still wants

to kill herself. So, that's that. I need to head to bed."

"She's being ridiculous," I hear Clarissa mutter.

I'm about to go ape shit and charge toward her but Evan catches me.

"Whoa, whoa, whoa," he says. "Let's just go to bed."

I push him away and storm off into my room, slamming my door. I can hear murmurs outside as I flop on the bed, cradling the wine bottle, my only true friend. A knock on the door and Evan enters, tip-toeing over.

"Nico…"

His body is warm as he gets under the covers with me. His beard has grown long and tickles the back of my neck.

"It just happened," he says. "We were at Max Fish and ran into her, and like, she's in a good place and so are we. There's no reason to have bad energy."

"She's cunning," I say, into my arm. "She wants to destroy us."

"No, no, she's in another band with these girls. They have–"

"A Samantha Fox kinda vibe, I know. I heard."

"Nico, don't let this get to you. Her and Lacey, I've seen them, they're happy."

"In all of three days?"

"They haven't left each other's side."

I flip over, facing him. "So, she's basically gonna move back in?"

"You can't police everyone. If Lacey and her are dating, then Lacey and her are dating."

"She's not even a lesbian!" I yell.

"Keep your voice down." He brushes my hair that has become sweaty from the heater and sticks to my face. "She swung both ways when we were dating too. It's not new for her. Swear. She's just an open person."

"Oh, I'm so glad she's such an open person."

"What do you want? For me to forbid her from coming in here? Lacey's her own person, she deserves to have a life. Nico, the Bouquets are soaring right now. That should be the focus. I know you just went through a lot—"

"This has *nothing* to do with Winter. You should have told me."

"I didn't want to upset you more. I didn't think you would run into them like this. I thought we'd get back and I could tell you discreetly."

I turn away from him again to the wall. I want to be alone. The bed is too hot with him in it and now it smells like beer.

"Nico..."

"Can you just...? I dunno, Evan, I wanna go to sleep."

"Okay."

"Alone. Like, I need my space."

He exits the bed that immediately gets chill without him. Now I want him back but I'm too embarrassed to say. He leans down to kiss the back of my head.

"Goodnight," he says. "I'm glad you're back."

He flips the light out as he leaves, and I want anything but to be alone now. I'm roiling with rage but so tired too, the wine pulling me toward sleep. I luckily reach it in moments, so I don't spend all night with my mind going through all the different ways Clarissa is primed to fuck us good. I ease into a sloppy dreamland, not realizing I'm squeezing my crystal penis tight until I wake up in the morning with it slicing into my palm.

27

• • • • •

I Alone – Live

'Ready to Guide' debuts on MTV's *Top 20 Countdown* at number twenty and the band gets invited on the show to do a spot with the VJ Daisy Fuentes, a bombshell in a vest and white tee with long brown hair and seductive eyes. She opens the show on a brown couch with a small audience watching from folding chairs.

"We've got a great top twenty for you this week with almost half of the songs by female artists, or bands fronted by a female singer. And we even have a special guest for you, the band Grenade Bouquets are here to talk about their latest album titled *Grenade Bouquets*. Then, will Green Day stay at number one with "Basketcase", or will they be knocked off their perch by Snoop Doggy Dogg's "Gin & Juice", or Boyz II Men's "I'll Make Love to You"? Lemme tell you, all of them could make love to me. Is that sharing too much? Haha, we're all friends. Anyway, kicking it off is Grenade Bouquets and their red-hot single "Ready to Guide". Are you ready to guide? I sure am."

I watch on the TV above as the number 20 flashes against a cream background with rainbow colors dripping over it like slime. And then there's our video. Starting out in the school auditorium before a class of barely interested students and then we get to thrashing. This is cut with me in the woods meeting my ghost. I'm lured further down pathways as it cuts back to Evan and I devouring each other on stage before my ghost leads me into the darkness and I disappear entirely.

We're then seated on another couch across from Daisy Fuentes, who crosses her legs holding onto her knee as if some serious journalism is about to occur.

"Wow, I got chills. Seriously, look at my arm."

Daisy shows it off as evidence.

"What was it like making that video?"

She's asking the band but she's looking directly at me, so I answer.

"Nels is amazing to work with," I say, licking my lips. I've put on heavy lipstick in a brown shade and wonder if I went too hard. I'm wearing a short dress that kinda looks like a tutu along with a choker and these lace gloves and my beaten-up Doc Martins for a vagabond vibe. "He's a real auteur," I continue. I heard that word in an interview recently when Brad Pitt was talking about the director David Fincher for their upcoming movie *Seven* and swore I'd use it in a sentence.

"So, I was saying that half the videos on our countdown today are from female singers or female fronted bands," Daisy says. "Do you see yourself at the beginning of a revolution, Nico?"

"Yeah totally, I mean, that's amazing. I have so

many women I've looked up to."

"Really? Who are some of your inspirations?"

"Uh, Courtney Love of course." I look over at the rest of the band, but they don't seem pleased. It's clear the interview is all about me. I can't worry about that now, though. "I love Shirley Manson of Garbage."

"'Only Happy When It Rains' is coming up on our countdown," Daisy says.

Oh Daisy, we're like two best friends just gabbing with each other.

"D'Arcy from Smashing Pumpkins," I say, nibbing on my lip. "Sleater-Kinney, L7, Babes in Toyland, Tori Amos."

"Do you find it's hard being the only woman in an all guy band?"

"Umm, these guys are great. They're like my family."

"She's that kid sister who's always getting you in trouble," Ed says, and gives a powerful laugh that Daisy ignores.

"That's what I mean," Daisy says. "You're the lead singer, but are you treated like a kid sister?"

Ed and Randy give me look that says they'll murder my bunny if I throw them under the bus.

"No, we like to joke around. It's all in good fun," I say.

"And if I'm correct, your boyfriend is in the band?"

Her eyes bat back and forth to Evan and I. He gets shy and starts up a thumb war with himself to occupy his nerves.

"Did you two start the band?" Daisy asks.

"No, no, definitely not," I say. "I joined Grenade Bouquets."

"But that's when you all got noticed, right?"

"No, I mean, yes, but not because of me. It was a coincidence."

"Nonsense, girl. You need to take ownership for your success. With a powerful voice like yours, that's what makes you stand out. And a pioneer."

"Wow, thank you." I'm gushing and don't even care to see how the rest of the guys are reacting.

"We're all pioneers…" Randy begins to say, but Daisy cuts him off.

"You heard it here, Grenade Bouquets and bad ass chick Nico Sullivan debuting at number twenty, but I imagine you'll be climbing those charts soon. And now at number nineteen, we have Live and "I Alone". I alone? Usually, it's with a bottle of wine and some brownie mix and the show *Friends*. Is that your alone?"

The TV above us shows the number nineteen before rainbow slime drips down and Live's "I Alone" appears. The audience claps. Daisy turns to me, puts her hand on my scabbed knee.

"That was great, Nico."

"Thanks so much."

"Thank you, guys, for doing that," Daisy says, but Ed and Randy get up without thanking her back and head off stage. Evan's still staring at his thumbs.

"Something I said?" Daisy asks, and then shrugs. "Men, right?"

"Can't live with them, can't live without them," I say, and then cackle like a hyena.

Daisy just smiles at that without showing her teeth. I take it as a cue to leave. As Evan and I walk off stage I ask him if I "monopolized that interview"?

"I mean, kinda," he says.

"But she, like, directed all the questions at me. What was I supposed to do?"

He pinches the bridge of his nose. "Lob some our way. Say, 'yeah it's female fronted but these guys are my brothers, and we make the music together. Ed for example…"

"I did. I did do that."

"Not really."

We reach the green room backstage. Ed and Randy are there, each halfway done with a bottle of beer.

"I'm sorry," I say. "Really. I'm new to these live interviews."

"This isn't your band, little girl," Randy says, pointing his Amstel at me. "Got it?"

"I get it."

He punches the wall. "It's fucking ridiculous is what it is. Like, the VJ didn't even look at me."

"I hear ya, brother." Ed clinks his bottle.

"Look, she knows now," Evan says. "We'll handle it differently. Spread the love around more."

"All the questions were asked to me," I say, opening my own beer and downing it. "You understand that's what makes us stand out, right? Do you know the names of the other guys in Garbage?"

"Butch Vig," Evan says.

I make a sound from my mouth that tells him he's not helping.

"All right, I'm sorry. I'm shit, I suck, crucify me." I give a Jesus pose. "Nail me to the wall. What do you want? We're on MT-fuckin'-V. Daisy Fuentes just interviewed us. Our song hit the top twenty. And you dicks are moaning about it. Be happy."

"Nah," Ed says. "I'm only happy when it rains."

"Oh, fuck off," I say, and make for the door. I give Evan a look to come, but he's focused on his twiddling thumbs. "And fuck you too, Evan."

"Wha…?"

"I'll get myself home."

I clutch the bottle and bolt out of the studios, hailing a cab outside in the snow.

"Where to?" the cabbie asks, a true New York cabbie of my dreams that might as well have a cigar burning from his lips.

"Can you just drive around?"

"It's your dime, doll."

"Can I smoke?"

"Again, your dime."

I roll down the window and light a cigarette, leaning out as the light snow kisses my eyelashes. I'm damn happy and if those assholes can't be, I'll find someone else to celebrate with.

"Stop here," I say, in front of a bar as I pay him and then get out my Sasha Lioni ID so I can get properly snockered, even if it's only past noon.

28

• • • • •

Glycerine – Bush

Our *Top 20 Countdown* appearance made us soar, the single not only moving up the radio charts but, even more importantly, creeping up MTV too. We passed Bon Jovi's "Always", and "U.N.I.T.Y", by Queen Latifah, the Gin Blossoms' "Hey Jealousy", and Meatloaf's "I'd Do Anything For Love (But I Won't Do That)" with just "Stay (I Missed You)" by Lisa Loeb keeping us out of the top ten. Grouch Records yanks us in for a meeting immediately to figure out the next single. I haven't really talked with the band much these last few days, trying to keep my distance, even from Evan. I started walking the city at night all the way down to the river and the Statue of Liberty with a joint in my hand and some wine sloshing around in my belly.

Part of me is pissed that Evan hasn't fought for me more. I know he thinks I need my space, and while I do, I'd melt if he came for a walk with me and said I mean more to him than the rest of the band. Maybe I'm still annoyed about Clarissa and how easily he let her back into our lives. Maybe I expect too much for him and this relationship.

On my last walk to view Lady Liberty before our meeting at Grouch, I think of what I want our next single to be. I know Ed and Randy are pushing for either "Sunny Side Down" or "Split", heavy songs that are probably our most Alice in Chainsy of the bunch. But looking at MTV's *Top 20 Countdown* there's very few grunge songs. I see hip-hop and pop and grunge-lite bands like Collective Soul and Oasis, maybe Radiohead, but not hard grunge like Nirvana was, or even Hole, it's more "alternative". For that reason, "Big Toe" might be our best bet. It has a Lisa Loeby kinda vibe and really showcases me and Evan. Even though I'm annoyed with him right now, I know he's got more talent than Ed or Randy, and the two of us created that song together. Maybe releasing it would solidify us as the center of Grenade Bouquets with Ed or Randy replaceable if they keep up their attitude.

At Grouch Records the next day, Terry Carbon is there with open arms and sushi platters.

"There's my stars," he says, clapping his hands and kisses on all of our cheeks. He smells of so much aftershave.

Liz Mesner gives us polite nods, all the congratulations we'd be getting from a cold fish like her. Speaking of cold fish, I'm starving so I get to eating the sushi.

There's bigwigs in the meeting who talk about our "career", so we wouldn't be only one song. How too many grunge bands had a minor hit and then were never really heard of again.

"We don't want to be a Tuesday's Bicycle," one

of them says.

"Who?" another one asks.

"Exactly."

"The point is we want to nurture you," the first one continues. "We planted the seed and now we want it to grow," he says, and continues with other lame metaphors. "So, let's spitball. What song are you thinking of next?"

He's looking directly at me, and I can feel the heat from the other guys beating down. My stomach's in knots and I'm about to pipe up but Ed beats me to it.

"'I'm thinking...we're actually thinking, 'Sunny Side Down'."

He's nodding around the table. Randy joins in, and Evan kinda nods, without really committing to it.

All the execs cock their heads to the right with a look that tells me *no.*

"We love 'Sunny Side Down', the only female exec chirps. "*Love* it. But it's so dark."

"So dark," the other says.

"Yeah, it's about rehab," Ed says, chewing on his lip, which means he's not pleased.

"Dark isn't 1995," one of the execs says, and turns to Terry Carbon who takes the baton.

"We're coming out of a recession," Terry Carbon says. "People want uplifting."

"But 'Ready to Guide'..." Randy says.

"Is uplifting," Terry Carbon adds. "Totally uplifting. It comes from pain, but it's about moving on. 'Sunny Side Down' feels stuck."

"'See-saw?' Randy says, because that's the song where he added the most input.

"Too…" the female exec begins. "What's the word I'm looking for?"

"Maudlin," another one adds, and they all agree.

"Nico," Terry Carbon says, his eyes boring into my soul. "We want to hear from you."

"You're the face of the band," another says.

I imagine Ed and Randy want to stab me with an axe, but I'm not gonna let them intimidate.

"'Big Toe'," I say plainly. I can see Evan's eyes go wide with surprise.

The execs all give us tiny smiles. "That's what we were thinking," they all say.

They explain how 'Big Toe' has a Lisa Loeb sound—*thank* you, exactly what I've been saying. And while it's not as hard and grunge as the rest of our songs, we have to consider our future.

I refuse to be a one and done band. I wanna be singing in my granny panties.

"So, we have no say?" I hear Ed argue and then Randy chimes in. Now they're fighting with the execs and I want out of the room. I'm flush and could use some water. I look to Evan who's leaning back in his chair, eyes glued to the ceiling. He doesn't want any part of the fighting.

"Hey," I whisper to him. "Hey."

He finally glances over. His eyes tell me he's over it, and maybe possibly me.

"What do you think?" I ask, again in a whisper.

He shrugs his shoulders.

"You have to have an opinion," I say.

"I dunno. I agree with the guys, I guess. I don't want to go softer. I'm sorry."

I get up and slam my chair into the table. Everyone stops arguing.

"I need…a minute."

I don't let anyone talk me out of it, just rush from the room. The hallway has blinding fluorescent lights that make me dizzy. Maybe it's a panic attack? "Glycerine" by Bush is quietly playing from the overhead speakers. Gavin Rossdale singing about an ending, a break-up. Is that where this is all headed for me too? I feel someone coming up behind me. Thankfully, Evan knows he needs to apologize.

"Evan," I say, turning around, but it's Terry Carbon.

"Nico," he says, his hands on my shoulders. "We're going with 'Big Toe'. Asking everyone in the band is a formality. We're ponying up the money. We call the shots. And I'm glad we're on the same page." His voice drops to a soothing lull. "You are the true talent. You know that don't you?"

"I dunno."

"Sssshhh." He's petting my hair, and even though it's weird, it calms me down. "Yes, you do. You were the one I noticed at that concert. Cold clocking that other girl, owning the stage. You have presence. They are serviceable. Your boyfriend more than the other two. He has talent, I'll give him that. But he needs way more confidence. You have your entire life ahead of you, one where you—and I—can become very rich."

"Oh."

"Listen to us, Nico. We know what's right. And we're on the same wavelength, you and I. You wanted 'Big Toe' as well."

"I did."

"Ssssh, calm yourself. They'll fall in line. Don't worry about them."

"Okay."

"My beautiful girl. My shining star."

He stops petting my hair. I let out a *woosah*, my hand firmly clamped on the crystal penis.

"'Big Toe'," he says, walking away.

"'Big Toe'," I say.

He fires a pretend gun at me with his fingers. "That's my quasar," he says. "Burning so bright." He gives me a wide grin showing me all his too white teeth. "Now let's go back inside. Tits out, chin up, show 'em who's boss. Like Tony Danza, *Who's the Boss?* You, Nico, it's you."

29

• • • • •

Fake Plastic Trees – Radiohead

We're shooting the video for "Big Toe" and I'm in hair and makeup. The director wants a softer look for me, less riot grrrl more debutante. The makeup is a light touch, mostly to enliven my cheeks and eyes. Since my hair is fried, there's not too much we can do with it, so the stylist slicks it back a la Robert Palmer. For a dress, I'm through with baby doll ones that have gashes. I'm given a floral number that a young English teacher would wear. It's pretty and goes down past my knees to cover up any scabs.

The shoot will mostly be with Evan and I. We're at a crossroads in our relationship—could it *be* any more on the nose, like Chandler Bing would say—and after a fight we're laying in bed barefoot and he's strumming his guitar and I kiss his big toe and it makes me remember all I love about him. How I was dead inside before and he brought me back to life. The scenes are cut with the band playing in the living room—we're renting an apartment in the West Village for the shoot that has a very *Friends*y vibe itself.

Both scenes will be difficult to film, way more than our last video. The director, Randall came from a movie background and is a stickler. He wants the band to start up mournful when me and Evan's relationship is at a low point and then become more joyful as our relationship gets better. The mournful part is easy, Ed and Randy have been sad dicks lately, groaning around the apartment about our "contract being unfair" and how "the band is a dictatorship". Evan's in the middle, but he tends to side with them. I guess there's a power in numbers. And Lacey's been M.I.A. since she's started up with Clarissa, so I don't even have her on my side.

"Your dress looks like a million flowers threw up on you," Ed says, in between a take. "Like are we the 10,000 Maniacs all of sudden? This song is so cheesy."

"Yes, Ed, you've made that known," I say, at my mic stand where I've been lip-syncing "Big Toe" all day, my jaw tired.

"It makes no sense either," he continues. "You're in a fight and then his big toe makes you realize how much you love him?"

Randy snickers in tandem. "So dumb."

"This is what the record execs want," I say. "You heard them at the meeting. I had nothing to do with it."

"Not buying it," Ed says.

"Me neither," Randy adds. "You put the bug in their heads."

"All right, guys," Randall the director calls out. "Let's do another take."

We go through the song, getting happier and happier, our smiles cartoonish. I catch a glimpse of myself

in a tall mirror and do look like Natalie Merchant, a
thirty-five-year-old lady as opposed to a bad-ass teen.
But they tell us that this is what our audience wants.
We're selling uplifting as opposed to slitting our wrists.

"Big toe, big toe
How I love you so
You taste of sweet milk
My lips like silk," I lip-sync.

Randall calls this part of the shoot. Ed and Randy
are done for the day, which means those two assholes
can get out of my face. They talk about getting bombed
at a bar on the corner, and I flee into the bedroom
where the lights are being set up.

Evan lies on the bed barefoot, a guitar in his lap.
He's strumming it and playing "Fake Plastic Trees" by
Radiohead, softly singing along, aping Thom Yorke's
whine and growl. I get on the bed next to him and sing
too, but we're not really grooving so I stop. I wonder if
I'm being fake by selling us out. If I'm more concerned
with pleasing Terry Carbon et al, rather than pleasing
someone I truly care about like Evan. A stylist comes
by and sprays mist in his hair to make it all spikey.

I look at his big toe tucked under his other leg. It
would be funny to lean down and kiss it right now,
make light of the situation, but he seems so glum,
glum, glum.

"Do you hate this song?" I ask, in a baby voice. I'm
scared to hear his reaction.

His eyes find the ceiling. "No, Nico, it's a very
pretty song..."

"But?"

"It's the album's closer, an aside. Something cute

between you and I. It's a mistake as a second single, no matter what *they* say."

"But why...?"

"Fans are fickle. They like the rawness of our first single, it's filled with rage. This is sweet and nice, but we'll lose them."

"Or gain other ones?"

"Maybe," he says, but I can tell he doesn't believe. Or he doesn't want those kinds of followers because we'll be losing cred. "What's the goal of all this?"

I pick at a Band-Aid on my elbow. "What do you mean?"

"Why are we doing this?"

A woman leans between us to touch up my hair and I have to lean around her to see him. "To make music? Be famous—"

"Who ever said I wanted to be famous?"

It's like someone let all the air out in the room. I feel flush and wish I could lie down on a pillow and go to sleep forever.

"Don't you...?"

"No, no I don't, Nico. I want to make music. I wanna tour the country with my friends and my girl. But this?" He gestures to all the people around us. "This is bullshit is what it is."

I'm about to give a lecture about all the money we're getting but stop myself because I know it'll only make things worse. He beats me to it.

"Do you just care about the money?" he asks, making a face like money equals sin.

"No! I don't. And fame... I mean, before I met you, I wasn't able to even sing in front of an audience. Like that was my dream, it is my dream! And traveling with you."

"Excuse me," Evan says to the woman primping my hair. "Could you give us...?"

She makes a face but gets out of our way.

"Then let's fuck all of this," he says, grabbing me close. He's strong and I feel safe.

"Fuck? What do you mean?"

"This, who needs 'em?"

"You mean Grouch Records, like we have a contract—"

"Rules, Nico, who makes these stupid rules we're supposed to follow?"

I'm speechless and that's not the answer he wants so he pulls away.

"Forget it," he says, picking back up his guitar. "Can we do the shoot already?"

Randall the director comes in and starts setting up the shot, so I don't have a chance to reply. I'm positioned on the bed, Evan's foot (and big toe) front and center. I'm told to begin from after the chorus.

"*Your quiet sleep*
My demon head
You have no worries
I dream of dead."

Evan and I lock eyes, saying so much to one another without really saying anything. He's disappointed with me, I'm frustrated with him. I know it's not cool to be a band all about fame and money, but like, why can't we have all of that? Why can't we make amazing music and for Evan and I to travel the world together and make a ton of money so we never have to work again, and leave behind a trail of beautiful music for generations and generations.

I look at his big toe. I still do love it so, even if it might not love me back anymore.

"*Big toe, big toe*
How I love you so
You taste of sweet milk
My lips like silk."

I give it a kiss. It's so cold it might as well have a toe tag.

"That's a wrap," I hear Randall the director say. The shoot is over. Before I can even turn to Evan, he jumps off the bed out of the room. I'm left alone as the crew leaves. It's nighttime and they close the lights on their way out.

I'm left in darkness, the moon such a sliver it gives off nothing.

30

● ● ● ● ●

Would – Alice in Chains

I'm morose and listening to "Would" by Alice in Chains while the rest of the band along with Lacey and stupid Clarissa are out partying at their local hangout Max Fish. I wasn't even invited. I went to get a Clearly Canadian from the bodega down the block and when I came back, they all were gone, seeing an opportunity to ditch my ass. I don't mind—I mean, I do, but the line has been drawn in the sand like the cliché says. I'm my own island and feeling sad. Playing Alice in Chains is one step away from opening a vein.

I call home but get both Mom and Dad's answering machines. It's around five o'clock in L.A. so they're likely still at work. Calling Jeremy, I get his mom who says he's on a field trip. She's also never been one for conversation. Jeremy has like five siblings and she's always chasing after them. Aunt Carly comes up empty too. Her machine says she's at some painter's retreat in Tahoe for the week. Good for her. All that's left in my Rolodex is Winter.

I'm hesitant to call. It's not like we left things so amazing the last time we spoke. And I'm looking for someone to make me feel better right now, not vice versa, which Winter is probably incapable of doing. But the CD starts to skip, and I have nothing else to do except crawl into a bottle of red, so I dial Winter's number and get Edina.

"Nico," she says, in her slurring way and I can tell she's inebriated too, my soulmate.

"Hi, Edina, how are you?"

"Oh, bloody good, ya-know. My sciatica says otherwise, but, well, that's fifty for you."

"How's Winter?"

She pauses for a sec, too long if you ask me and my stomach gets squirmy. "She's back at home, in school too."

She wisely doesn't lie that she's doing great.

"Can I speak to her?" I ask, my voice soft like I'm afraid of the answer.

"Let me find out."

I can sense her winking at me through the receiver, like she has my back. She disappears and when she returns, her voice has a smile behind it.

"She's about to head out but will pick up. Darling, we're so proud of you. Saw your video on the TV."

"Thanks, Edina."

I'm getting weepy. Maybe it's the wine or hearing from someone in my life who cares. It seems lately like I have no one. I want to vent to her about Evan and the rest of the band, but then Winter picks up.

"Ma, hang up," I hear her yell and then the sound of a click. "Hey."

"Hey."

I'm twirling the phone cord around my finger like a little girl waiting to hear if the guy she likes will ask her out.

"You're home?"

"Is that a question?" Winter asks.

"No, I…"

"I'm just fucking with you, Nico. Yeah, I'm home, whoop-dee-do."

"It must be better than there."

"That's like saying it's better not to be fucked gently with a chainsaw," she says, mimicking our favorite *Heathers* quote. I laugh.

"Oh, Heather, what's your damage?"

"So, I was about to head out the door," Winter says. "Really."

"Where are you going?"

"Um, seeing this dude."

"Ooooh, care to share?"

"He was Emily's guy."

"You still hanging with Emily Valentine?"

"That skank? Yeah, no. But I am seeing her guy, just to twist the knife in."

"Is it working?"

"Yeah, she throws daggers at me with her eyes all day every day. And I'm still seeing Don."

"Wait? Don, the dude who…?"

"Nico, please don't lecture me."

"No, I'm not. You can see whoever you want."

"I will. I am. Sometimes I see them on the same night. I dunno, it keeps me from being bored."

"Yeah."

There's a lull in the conversation. It's like we on two different planets. Her choices are terrible, but it's not like mine have been so amazing. I've been shitting the bed in terms of my own relationship. And my drinking... well...

"I saw your video," Winter says. "It's cool."

"Really?" I'm gushing to get her approval. "Like, I know it's not Marilyn Manson."

"No, it's not, but it's your own thing, I guess. You're a bad ass chick in that video. Kissing your man so hard you make his lip bleed, frolicking with your ghost."

"If he is my man anymore."

"What? Really?"

"We're having issues. Me and the rest of the band. They're not happy with the second single, it's slower and the spotlight's all on me."

"Fuck them, Nico. Look, you can't please everyone, right?"

I hear her sucking at what's likely a joint and miss getting high with her, a true friend even though we've had beef. I take a swig of an old bottle of wine on the dresser drawer. It's so warm it almost tastes like puke.

"I'm pleasing no one right now. I'm sorry, I don't want to complain. Like that's so annoying of me. How are you? Really?"

She lets out a long breath. "You mean, do I think of swallowing more pills?"

"I..."

"Nico, that was, like, a moment. Do you ever have a moment? I reacted. It was stupid. I went through counseling. Blah, blah, blah. Don and Zedd's daily dick sessions are enlivening my spirits."

"Zedd?" I say, bursting out in laughter. "As is, 'Zedd's dead, baby'?"

"How good was *Pulp Fiction*?"

"I've seen it twice," I say. "Once at the Angelika with Evan..."

I think about that day when we were so in love and it seemed like nothing could come between us. A few months and a lifetime ago.

"I care about him," I say, mostly to myself.

"Well, then get him back, girl," Winter says. "Whatever it takes."

"Yeah. You know, I'm sorry."

"For what?"

"For what happened to us, Wint. I mean, I was afraid to call."

"Oh yeah, whatever. I mean, I don't let shit stew, ya-know. I was pissed at you, you were pissed at me, we'll be pissed at each other again. Benny Bear's been keeping me company. When he doesn't steal my cigs that is."

Tears are dripping down my cheeks. "I miss you."

"I miss you too, Nic. Especially now that I've given Emily the boot and Jeremy's so busy. He got an after-school job at a salon and all he talks about is hair, hair, hair. He did mine though, it's good."

"What's it look like?"

"Would you believe I have dreds like the 4 Non Blondes chick? Winter colored of course."

"What? I'm on the floor!"

"I'm getting used to them. It's nice not to have to wash my hair all the time. Sometimes I chew on them..."

"Which is gross."

"Yeah, which *is* gross. Whatever. Okay, I really have to go. I hear Zedd's hog revving up on the street. We're going to this thing in the Tar Pits, this biker thing."

"Sounds cool."

I've been smiling the whole time, feeling way less *Alice in Chains*y than I did before I called.

"Toodles," she says.

I want to tell her I love her and always will, but don't wanna push it. We inched closer together this conversation, and that's enough for now.

"Toodles," I say, and hang up.

I grab the bottle of wine and spill the rest. I realize Winter and I could fight with our claws out but then find a way to get back to normal with one another. Like sisters would.

And while I'm not jazzed with her weird *menage a trois* biker relationship, she sounded more like the Winter I love than she has in a long time, and I'll take that as a win for now. In fact, I'm gonna go to bed early before this night has any chance of turning.

I get into PJs like a little girl, leave a lava lamp on, and I'm asleep in an instant, for the first time in a while without allowing any worries to infiltrate my mind.

31

• • • • • •

Cannonball – The Breeders

"Big Toe" is released with a heavy amount of promo but managed to only debut at number 49 on the *Billboard* Alternative Rock chart. With 'Ready to Guide' peaking at number 9 and still at 32, it's considered a flop. The video doesn't do much better. We play an acoustic spot for MTV to build excitement and don't even make their *Top 20 Countdown*. No more Daisy Fuentes interviews for us. Fingers start pointing immediately.

Terry Carbon blames Liz Mesner for the wrong kind of publicity. The execs shrug it off, since alterna bands (as we're called) have a hard time with sophomore singles after *minor* first hits. It's the way they say "minor" that gets me in the gut. A few weeks ago, we were the bee's knees to them, now we're an afterthought.

The massive tour planned gets cut to a few dates. A third single is discussed but as an aside in a "sure, we'll get to that" kind of speak that leads me to believe they might not even get behind a third single.

A bulk of the money we're due is also contingent on album sales (something Lacey negotiated), and since the album won't be climbing the sales charts anytime soon, we likely won't hit that golden number. So, to sum up, everyone's pissed at Lacey because they think she made a shit deal (and has been off in La La Land with Clarissa), everyone is *certainly* pissed at me for suggesting "Big Toe", Ed and Randy are miffed at Evan for not "keeping me under control", (actual words from Ed's stupid fat mouth), Evan is avoiding me so he doesn't get shit from Ed or Randy, who've been on obnoxious drunken benders, Terry Carbon won't return my calls, we've gotten tons of hate mail calling us posers and sellouts and begging us to kill ourselves, and I'm getting bombed listening to The Breeders' "Cannonball", pretending like my life hasn't turned into a sewer drain.

I'm interrupted by what sounds like a tussle outside of my room. Stepping outside, I find Ed, Randy, and Evan involved in some weird wrestling move. Through my inebriated understanding, it seems as if Ed and Randy are off their rocker and taking out their anger on Evan, who's just trying to defend himself. Lacey and Clarissa run out of Lacey's room half-naked and gawk at the spectacle. I dive in to fix the situation.

"Enough! Stop!"

I get an elbow to my face and bite down on my tongue, which gushes blood.

"Fuck, really?"

Ed's fat elbow is the culprit, so I punch him in the belly. He goes down hard.

"Awww, Nico."

He's rolling around on the floor and pukes a little. Randy gets in my face with some misogynistic slurs.

"You wanna be on the floor too?" I yell at him. Somehow, he wades through his drunkenness and steps back, holding up his hands.

We're all catching our breath. Evan's face has been bruised from their knuckles.

"Shit," I say, touching his split lip. "Why are you fighting?"

"Why do you think we're fighting?" Randy says, eyeing me like he wants to murder my first born. "It's you, Nico."

Ed pukes again in front of all of our feet.

"Gross," I say, jumping away so I don't get sprayed.

"We had a vision," Ed says, wiping his mouth. "And you ruined it."

"You all weren't going anywhere," I say. "You were playing small gigs and would have stayed that way. I got Terry Carbon's interest."

"Yeah, because he wants to tap that," Randy says.

Evan punches him in the face hard, causing Randy to almost fall over.

"That's wrong, man," he says. "Seriously wrong."

Ed shakes his head. "That dude's had his eyes on your girl the whole time."

Evan charges at Ed. "You take that back."

They square up, Ed with about fifty pounds on Evan so it's no match.

"Stop it, stop it!" I get between them again and take another elbow to my face, this time Evan's.

"I'm sorry, I'm sorry," he says, turning toward me while Ed cold clocks him and Evan goes down.

"Evan!"

I'm hovering over and slapping his cheeks as he vacillates between unconsciousness.

"What is wrong with you all?" I scream.

Randy lights a cigarette. "You're what's wrong, Nico. It's always been you. I'll say this, we didn't have these types of problems when Clarissa was the singer."

Clarissa gives a smug shrug and I leap up to attack her.

"No, Nico, no," Lacey cries, and now us three girls are locked into a tussle. I have Clarissa's hair in my fist, which is a shady way to fight, but I don't care. She's screeching like a loon and I'm taking my frustration out on her. I get in one good punch before we're broken up.

"Screw you, Nico," Lacey yells, with hate in her heart. She looks at me like she never wants to see me again, hugging Clarissa close as she weeps.

"I'm outta here," I say. I find someone's boots lying around and another person's jacket and I'm out the door. It's night, I don't even know what time, and I'm shivering because it's like late March and under the jacket I'm only wearing a bra and short shorts. I luckily find a loose cigarette in the pocket along with a lighter and rip into it, smoking over half the cig in one long puff.

I hear patters from down the empty street as Evan catches up to me in just a T-Shirt. He's rubbing his jaw. I collapse into his chest, sobbing and overwhelmed.

"They're so cruel," I say.

He's rubbing his jaw. "Yeah, they really are dicks."

My snotting is endless, all over his shirt. "It's not like I set out to destroy the band. 'Big Toe' was meaningful, it was about us. I thought people would love it."

"Fans, man, you can never please everyone."

"You came to my defense tonight."

He takes my face in his hands. "Of course, Nico, I still care about you."

"But I've ruined everything."

"We're all wasted, none of us are making sense."

"Your lip." I touch the blood. "Your jaw."

He gives a lopsided smirk. "Yeah, I have some battle scars."

"You hate me, I know you do."

"I don't hate you."

"They're right," I say, throwing away the cigarette. "You guys had your path and I derailed it. I do that. I blow shit up. Maybe it would've better if you never met me."

He lets go of me now, blinking hard. "Don't say that."

"It's true. You would've been happily playing gigs and not in this mess. I make messes."

"I like my life a little messy. You add flavor."

"I just want to find a bar right now and crawl into the bottom of a glass."

He holds my arm. "Nico, let's go back—"

"Oh no, I am *not* going back there. At least while they are all still awake."

"All right, I'll come with—"

"No," I say, pushing him away. While I long to be close to him, I don't want to talk anymore. I'm exhausted. The dreams I had for our success will never happen now, and nothing he could say will make me feel better.

"Man, you're so hot and cold, Nico. I don't know what to do with you."

"That's right, you don't," I say, venomous. "You never have."

"Now you're just saying shit."

"I don't want to do this right now, Evan. Just go." And when he doesn't, I raise my voice. "Just, GO!"

He throws up his hands. "I can't win with you. Here I go to bat for you—"

"I didn't ask you to. Fuck, I DO NOT want to do this right now." I stamp my foot. "I just want to numb."

"Yeah, get so drunk you fall asleep in your puke. That's you on the regular."

This stings like a million bees are going to town on my heart.

"Maybe it is. Maybe that's all I am."

"You're not making sense."

"Because I don't want to make sense. Just leave me alone, Evan."

His baby blues reflect back only sadness. I've hurt him again, something I do well. It's easier for me to be vicious than vulnerable.

I'm walking backwards and he's standing there. I want to rewind the last few minutes but know that even if I did, I'd lose him again in some way. Because I'm a time bomb, I'm a cannonball, I destroy everything around me and know that deep down I enjoy those explosions, the power I can hold. With everything seeming like it's slipping away, it's all I have.

So, I'm running down the street to get as far away from him and sanity as possible. And I'm partly thrilled because I know how much it hurts him and I'm a monster like that. At a bar, thank Jesus they don't ask for my Sasha Lioni ID since I don't have it on me. I order Long Island Iced Teas and tell the bartender to keep them coming. I have no money on me, but he doesn't need to know that. It'll only be a terrible end to what has already been a terrible night. All I can relish in is to feel sorry for my pathetic self.

Without fame and fortune, what else do I have? What's the point? A thought infiltrates that my life may have peaked. I drown that thought in another Long Island Iced Tea, but it lingers, picks at my brain, feeds on my insecurities.

I know even when I wake up very hungover, it still won't have let go.

Primed to destroy my soul.

32

• • • • • •

Lightning Crashes – Live

I'm talking to this rando dude in the bar after three L.I. Iced Teas and I think he's hot, but it might only be my beer goggles. I know he's older, certainly not turning nineteen like Evan, but *older* older. But if Winter could be with mature guys, then why can't I? He has a nose ring and I tell him it's cool and we laugh, laugh, laugh. He touches my thigh and I let him. He tells me I'm beautiful and I let him. When he suggests getting out of here, I say I live not too far and let him pay my tab so I can get out of having to wash the dishes.

Down the street we're making out and he does this jab, jab thing with his tongue. He tastes like every kind of alcohol imaginable with a hint of tobacco and people are giving us looks. "Screw you," I tell them, my middle finger in the air. He says I'm a "wild spirit" and I reply that he "doesn't even know".

"I'm a Rockstar," I say. "At least I still am today."

"Oh yeah?" I realize he has a big bushy mustache

and I have a little bit of puke in my mouth but manage to keep it down. He's wearing a jeans vest and I use that to pull him into the apartment. In a haze, I see the rest of the band is still up, even though it's like four in the morning. They're sitting around the table in the kitchen.

"This is…"

I'm searching through my mind for this dude's name, but I can't find it.

"Jason," he says.

"Of course it is." I point at all the Bouquets. "Jason, these are my bandmates, the bunch of assholes."

"Hey, Bunch of Assholes, cool name for a band." Jason's smile tickles his mustache in a way that I now find cute.

"Go to bed, Nico," one of them replies.

"You go to bed!"

I trip over something and Jason catches me in his arms.

"So gallant," I say, and kiss him hard.

"Don't let Evan see," I hear another one of them say.

"What?" I shout. "Of course, Evan should see. Evan! Evan!"

I'm banging on pots and pans until a sleepy Evan emerges from down the hall in pajamas bottoms. He's digging his palm into one of his eyes.

"What is it?" he yawns, taking in the Jason situation. "Nico, what are you doing?"

"We—meaning he and I—are boning tonight. So there."

"So there," Jason mimics.

"Nico, don't do this," Evan whines.

"Oh, I am *so* doing this, doing him. All night."

"Forget her, Evan," I think Ed says, and Randy possibly echoes.

"You all are *so* superior," I say. "Because you are, what, a year and half older than me? B.F.D. You're no different. We're all damaged."

As I pass Evan, he grabs my arm. "You don't have to do this," he says, so tired.

I'm baring my teeth. "Yes, I do."

Maybe I want him to fight more for me, even though that's a messed-up thing to ask. Who else would've had that kind of patience? But nothing seems like it matters anymore. We're on the downward spiral. Everything's pointless.

"Let's talk," he says.

"Mate, I think you wanna step aside," Jason says.

Wait, is Jason British? I hadn't noticed that before, but now he totally has an accent. I'm going international, folks.

"She's seventeen," Evan says, bumping him with his chest.

"I'm eighteen in a few months," I say, bumping into them both. "So scurry back to your bedroom, bub, because I'm fine."

"She is fine," Jason says, with a slick grin. "A lady knows what she wants."

"She certainly does." I yank Jason by his jeans vest again. "C'mon."

I stare Evan down as we go past. His blue, blue eyes aren't sad anymore, just spent. The energy zapped through his skin. He doesn't try to stop us, so I go into my room with the Brit and slam the door.

I turn on the light and Jason looks even older, so I shut the light. The moon coats the room, our faces in blue. I turn on my boombox where my mixtape has stopped on "Lightning Crashes" by Live. I'm singing along softly as Jason begins to take off my clothes. I want to tell him to stop, but I've come this far. I couldn't go outside and face the Bouquets again.

I'm safe here, I tell myself.

He's on top of me on the bed, and I try to pretend he's Evan but it's too hard. Jason is thick where Evan is slim. Jason is greedy where Evan is giving. I'm kissed in a way that I feel like meat instead of a princess. I stare at the ceiling instead, the shadows moving across, "Lightning Crashes" reaching its chorus. I could've easily had Evan with me right now. We wouldn't even have to make love; he could've just held me. But I chose this path, this darkness.

Brit Jason finishes rather quickly with a grunt before the song has even ended.

"Thanks, Rockstar," he whispers in my ear, along with a belch that smells like he dined on olives.

"Don't go," I say, because he's already putting back on his jeans vest.

"It's late," he says, looking at his wrist but he has no watch.

"No, don't let them see you." I'm in tears, shaking my head, the sheets wrapped around my body like a toga.

"Ah, I get you." He fires a pretend gun at me. "I'll head out the fire escape."

"Thank you," I say, even though I have no clue what I'm thanking him for.

And then he's gone without even a goodbye, a cold

wind whipping into the room. I lean out the window, but he's not on the street leaving me to wonder if he was ever even here. I look upward and see that the fire escape also leads to the rooftop.

Maybe it's time for me to escape too?

33

• • • • •

Sick of Myself – Matthew Sweet

Somehow in pursuit of the fire escape that I imagined twisted up into heaven, I managed to put on my baby doll dress, the one I wore when Terry Carbon first noticed us and said he'd make us stars. I grabbed a bottle of Absolut Citron and a pre-rolled joint along with the crystal penis Aunt Carly gave me as I climbed to the sky. When Winter swallowed too many pills, she spoke of it as a moment, and I realize that's what depression can do. She's been diagnosed, and while I never have, I feel it churning inside at times, crawling on top of me and exerting enough pressure that I can't ignore it anymore. I'm having a moment and moments can be dangerous.

The roof deck is only three stories up, but enough to make an impact. The pot and alcohol fueling my system, goading me to jump as I murmur the chorus to "Sick of Myself" by Matthew Sweet. There's a light rain in the night and I'm barefoot and my toes are so cold. Right now, I'm so empty it's the only thing I feel. I think of Kristen. What it must have been like in her moment before death. Did she see it coming? Creeping up and filtering throughout her body before it attacked her brain? A star twinkles and I think of it as her eye watching. Is this what she would want for me? Definitely not.

With that thought, I slip and knock my head against the tarred roof. Flitting in and out of consciousness, my life truly passes before my eyes—this entire journey. From when I started touring with Grenade Bouquets, to usurping Clarissa as the main singer, to getting signed by Grouch Records, to playing venues and hearing fans scream my name, to Daisy Fuentes on MTV. And then the spiral: the constant hangovers, the thirst for any type of alcohol when I'm not drinking, the endless fighting with the band, and Evan, of course Evan, how I'd push him away when he'd get too close, how I wouldn't allow him to be anything other than perfect. A few minutes ago, I let some old dude inside of me whose name I can't even remember, just to spite Evan. I don't even know who I am anymore.

As unconsciousness takes over, I see Evan running toward me, shouting my name, pure anguish destroying his face. He's picking me up, checking my pulse, calling for help. I'm a slain bride in his arms until he's eclipsed by darkness. Maybe I'm dead. If I am, I deserve it, since I took this life for granted. If I wake, I promise to change, promise to get help, promise to be a better Nico. For Kristen and all she wasn't able to do with her own life. And for myself too since I'm only a sapling and have lifetimes ahead of me if I choose that path.

***

I wake to horrible fluorescent lights with an IV in my arm and crappy sheets chaffing my ass. I know this place well. Last year, I took a pill and got behind a wheel and banged my head, winding up in a hospital too. Rinse, repeat. Score, Nico.

"Hello?" I say, but no one is there. Last time, Evan was there to greet me with tears in his eyes. This time, no one gives a shit.

I push the call button and a nurse arrives. She's as old as God, unimpressed with my recovery.

"Oh, you're up?" she says, checking my vitals with a shrug.

"What happened? Was I in a coma?"

"An alcohol and doobie coma," she declares, pulling up my sheet and frowning when she sees I've wet the bed. "No, you weren't in a coma."

I touch the back of my skull. "My head?"

"Yeah, you got a lump. It'll heal."

"Is anyone here for me…?" I ask, but she's already out the door. She returns with fresh sheets and maneuvers me around while she fits them over the plastic mattress. "I asked if anyone was here for me?"

"I heard ya."

She tosses the pissy sheets in a bin and leaves. Minutes pass and I'm about to hit the call button again when Evan comes inside.

He looks like hell. Obviously, he hasn't slept. Rings take up residence under his eyes, his nose raw possibly from crying.

"Déjà vu?" I say, trying to be funny. He doesn't smile.

"Jesus, Nico."

"I know, I know." I slap my hand. "I was stupid. I'm stupid, what I can say?"

He comes over to the side of my bed, seeming like he's afraid.

"Are you okay?"

"Yeah, the nurse seemed totally unaffected by me waking up, so I'm thinking it's not too serious."

"It is serious."

"No, I know, I'm in a hospital. I mean, not life threatening or anything."

He sighs in a way that tells me I'm a nuisance.

"I'm sorry you have to deal with this," I say, taking a sip of water because my throat is so dry. My head actually hurts to move. "How did you know I was up on the roof?"

He removes my crystal penis from his pocket, now broken in half.

"You left this on the fire escape." He places it on the bedside table and pulls up a seat. "We need to talk."

"That guy..." I say. "I don't know what I was thinking. He didn't mean anything."

"I'm quitting Grenade Bouquets."

I do a spit take with the water like I'm in a *Seinfeld* episode.

He strokes his flesh-colored beard. "I'm not happy. And music is like the one thing I truly love to do, ya-know? I don't want it to feel like a chore."

I breathe in, receiving this wild information. "Yeah...no, I get it."

"It's the band, it's you, it's the fame, it's the record company, it's everything. It's not what I imagined it to be."

I'm fighting the tears to stay in my ducts. "Me neither."

"And we got a call from Grouch Records this morning. They're cutting even more dates and balking on a new single, but like they won't budge with their contract. It's like they're eating us alive, and I wanna walk away."

I swallow and it seems like it takes eons for it to go down. "I'm sorry, I know it's all me—"

"It's not, Nico. Well, a lot is you. You're... I love you—"

I wanna shout to the entire hospital that I love him too.

"But I'm not sure we're good for each other. In a relationship, you want your partner to bring out the best in you, right? I feel like sometimes we bring out the worst in each other. Like it's a game of sorts."

I'm wincing because this is so true.

"So as much as I like you, as much fun as you I have, and the awesome music we created together, I dunno, I think it's best if we just..."

I take his hand. Mine looks so pale with an IV stuck in a throbbing vein.

"I blow shit up," I say, nodding. "Always have, maybe always will. Maybe I like the drama? Maybe I'm not interesting enough without it?"

"That's not true."

I shrug, taste my tears. "You deserve better. With me, with the band. You deserve everything you've ever wanted."

"You say that like you don't?"

I keep shrugging. "I have a lot of issues I think I've been ignoring. Like, depression and stuff. Not even related to Kristen. It's always been there, even if I've tried to pretend like it isn't."

He leans over and kisses my forehead. "I wanna be there for you, Nico."

"No, you don't have to. Really, Evan. I've caused enough damage."

"Even as a friend. Anytime you need it. I'm gonna head back to Oregon."

My heart's been torn asunder, shreds of it littering the hospital floor. I'll pick it up later, once he's gone, when I'll allow myself to fully collapse.

"Ed and Randy too, they're breaking contract as well. So, Grenade Bouquets is officially kaput. I'm not gonna do something with them either. I'm not really sure I want them in my life. I'm thinking I'll go on a walkabout or something. The weather's getting warmer, and I'll hike with no destination, but really with every destination. Sounds like it might be exactly what I need."

Now I collapse, unable to hold it in anymore. I've loved this boy, unlike I've ever loved someone before, and I wonder if I ever will again? The thought brings me chills. He sees me breaking apart and hugs me tight.

"I want you to promise me to ease up on the drinking," he says. "Go home, be with your family, go back to school and get a degree. Like, I shouldn't have let you drop out."

I'm shaking in his arms. "Okay."

"Really promise me, Nico." He's looking in my eyes now and his are so blue, two perfect swimming pools. "You are amazing."

"Stop."

"You are. You're a star. And maybe that'll still be your path. You want it. I know you do. Maybe now is just not the right time."

I don't know what I want. If I'm more upset at the thought of the band ending or losing him. It's so many emotions all at once I don't know how to deal. I should tell him I love him, that maybe we simply need some time apart, but my lips are frozen. His baby blues look away. The old as God nurse has entered the room with a bedpan.

"It's time for her to empty her bowels," she says, clinking the bedpan with her sharp nails.

Way to ruin a moment, lady!

"Oh, okay," Evan says, stepping away.

"No." I'm reaching out but he's already backing up. The nurse nods for him to continue out of my life for good.

"I'll check in with you," he says. "At your folks'. After my walkabout. Yeah, yeah, okay, Nico. Bye."

"I love you," I finally say, but he's already gone, so it's as if I'm declaring it to the old nurse. She purses her lips in response.

"Scooch up so I don't have to clean these sheets too," she says, shoving the bed pan under me. I can barely see her from the tears blurring my vision.

"You know, I can make it to the bathroom."

She snarls. "Can you?"

"Yes," I say, pushing the bed pan away so it clangs on the floor. I go to get up, but I'm still attached by IVs.

"See," she says, with a wicked smile. "Now are you ya gonna scooch up again, or are we gonna have a real problem?"

"Problems are all I know," I say, picking my butt up as the cold pan touches flesh and a true love walked out of my world for good.

All that I have left is myself. And I've been sick of myself like the song says for a long, long time.

"Let me know when you've emptied," the nurse says, checking her watch.

"I'm empty. Totally empty."

34

• • • • •

Streets of Philadelphia – Bruce Springsteen

I flee back to L.A., my tail between my legs. I don't come out of my room for days, Mom leaving plates outside my door. She wisely lets me mourn. With the rest of the band quitting, Grouch Records cancels our contract. Any money we made, or will still make, goes to recouping their loss for the pulled dates. But I'm really missing Evan like the deserts miss the rain. I'm listening to our CD over and over, not to remember when we're we on top of the charts but for hints of him. Each pluck of his guitar burned to memory, his vibrato in the background, our voices together. On repeat softly at night when I go to sleep, the CD never leaves my boombox. Finally, one morning I emerge.

Mom looks at me strangely, pours a bowl of Fruit Loops. I watch the milk turn this weird brown from all the colors. She gives me as much advice as she can, but I've experienced something she hasn't, so she soon stops. All she can give me is time. Dad's the same. He talks of going back to school like college could duplicate stardom. When I tell him it's not about that, he's even more confused. His squeeze, Annette knows better. "It's about a boy," she tells him. Aunt Carly invites me to Ojai for a cleanse, but I'm only in the mood to stew. I don't want to feel better. I want to stay stuck in my filth. So I decline. She says the door's always open when I'm ready.

I haven't talked to Winter, haven't even really left my house, when I get a call from her.

She whispers, sounding covert. "Nico, can you come over?"

"Hey, Wint. Yeah, I haven't taken a shower since... what day is it today?"

She's crying. Winter never cries. She's a statue. I sit up in bed, my heart murmuring. I can hear it thump.

"I need you," she says. "Please."

She hangs up without saying anymore. I step in front of the mirror, my hair in electro-shock mode, my shirt looking stained with baby food, a dusting of hair under my arms. I throw on a Dodgers cap and an LL Bean fleece my dad once got me from the outlet store.

When I get to Winter's, Edina is surprised to see me.

"I didn't know you were home," she gushes. "Are you on tour, darling?"

"Mom, she'll talk to you later!" Winter screams from her room.

Edina shrugs. "She's in a tizzy all right. Don't know what it can be. Go do the Lord's work."

I smile and head down the hallway. I have this prickling sensation all over my body, like when you know an electronic device is on in another room. I hear Bruce Springsteen's "Streets of Philadelphia" coming from under Winter's doorjamb until it stops suddenly.

Inside Winter sits crossed-legged on the bed, mascara tears dripping from her eyes. Her hair is dreadlocked like she said and actually looks hella good. She's wearing a sleeveless T-shirt from a Screaming Trees show we went to last year where we drank too much DayQuil.

"Nico," she says.

I'm on the bed with her, unsure whether she wants a hug. "What is it?"

I'm looking to see if she's physically hurt by one of her dudes. I wouldn't be surprised. She wipes her eyes until her palms are stained black.

She's rocking back and forth. "I can't believe it."

"What? Winter, you're freaking me out."

She tips her head back, lets out a grunt like she's possessed. It gives me chills.

"Okay, you know Don?" she asks, and then gives a snarl. "That asshole Don?"

"The biker guy? Yeah, what happened?"

"So, like, I've been with him the last few months, you know. And Zedd too, fuck I have to call Zedd."

She's using, I can tell. Her eyes are all spacey, her words herky-jerky. It's not from pot because the room doesn't smell like weed. I scan for little bottles, but don't see any—I could use a drink. I found some cherry cordial in Mom's cabinet earlier that I sipped. Which means Winter's on something harder.

She grabs the phone. "I can't even remember his number right now." She flops back on the bed, throws her hands over her face. "Ugh."

I take the phone away from her like she might hurt herself with it.

"Winter, calm down. Just tell me what happened."

She pops back up. "Okay, so, Don, like the other day we're at this bonfire on Hermosa Beach, and he's being all quiet, I mean, he's a man of few words, but he's like being really weird, and so I'm like, Don, what's up, and he's all, I went to doctor the other day, and I'm like okay, whatever, and then he's like, yeah for a test, and I'm all, what test, and he goes, well, Sandy got tested, and I'm like, who the fuck is Sandy, and I'm thinking she's pregnant, like he got some random ho pregnant, so I'm like, I know you're cheating on me, and he goes, that's not the issue, and I tell him about being with Zedd, who's his friend, and he says he doesn't care about Zedd, he got tested, and I'm like, what fucking test are you talking about, and he goes, for HIV, Winter, I got tested for HIV, and I'm like what, and he says, yeah I got tested, and I have it, I have HIV, and so I'm going crazy because we were like together a lot, and I didn't use condoms, I've never been into condoms, I'm on the pill, like Edina's always gotten me the pill since I was like fourteen and so I'm like what should I do, and he says *get tested*, and like I can't Nico, I'm too afraid to go...and...take...a...test..."

All the words have been zapped from my body. It's as if she's telling this to me and I'm hovering above, watching it all play out. She gushes tears and I warn myself to find the strength to be present. I engulf her with a massive hug. She's moaning on my shoulder and I'm stroking the back of her head and I don't know what I'm saying. I'm frozen popsicle. AIDS had been drummed into us since elementary school. In health class we were warned about not using a condom, and

I remember Winter making a joke. An art teacher at school contracted it along with a kid I barely knew who wound up leaving. We all watched *Philadelphia* with Tom Hanks and learned about lesions. We understood when Pedro from *The Real World* explained how it was safe for him to be a roommate to seven strangers. We decorated bags for God's Love We Deliver, but that was the extent of the disease, it existed on the outskirts of our lives. Now it hit home.

"Does Edina know?" I hear myself asking.

"No. Oh shit, and Zedd, I gotta tell Zedd."

She goes to pick up the phone again, all cried out.

"How many ways can I screw my life up?" she asks, almost with a laugh.

My problems seem miniscule, the true gravity of the situation not even kicking in yet.

"Jeremy?" I ask.

"He doesn't know either. You were the first."

"I'm so sorry, Winter. I don't...I don't know what to say."

"Like, I know I have it, how could I not? How could I be so fuckin' stupid? And to trust this guy? This asshole."

"He's such an asshole."

"How can I take this test and wait for an answer, and like hear the nurse tell me I have AIDS? I can't even deal with it."

"Okay, okay, Winter, you don't know for certain." She's fighting in my arms, squirming around like hella crazy.

"Yes, yes I do. I can feel it in inside me. I know!"

"Listen," I say, taking charge. "Winter, listen!" I

hold her arms to her sides so she can barely move. "You do *not* know. Okay? It's not certain. We'll go get a test. There's that Planned Parenthood in Van Nuys. My car is outside."

"Nico, I'm so scared."

"I am too. I'm really scared, and I love you, and I'm mad at your choices, and it's been an insane last few weeks, but you cannot be sick, do you hear me? I am not going to accept that. You're okay, I know you're gonna be okay."

"Do you think so? Really?"

"Let's get you tested. Here, you need flip-flops." I scurry around the room, wiping the snotballs from my nose, finding her flip-flops and putting them on. "And here's your hoodie, okay, let's get it on you."

"Okay," she sniffles.

I direct her into a hoodie and lead her out of the room. Edina is there with a *what's going on?* look, so I mouth, "It's about a boy."

"Ah," she says, and mimes hanging herself.

I get Winter to my car, put her in shotgun, fasten her seatbelt. She's gone numb now, just mumbling. We drive to Van Nuys and I'm her life coach, saying over and over that "everything is going to be ok". I'm repeating it to myself too. For the implosion of Grenade Bouquets and mine and Evan's relationship, for the chance that I could lose Winter to AIDS.

At Planned Parenthood, a kind nurse takes Winter into a room and allows me to come inside. I'm holding Winter's hand as the nurse draws blood. I'm singing her favorite Pearl Jam song because I don't know any Marilyn Manson. She sings along as she winces from the needle. We're told it can take up to a week to get results.

"Will you stay with me until I hear?" Winter asks, when we're back in the car.

"Of course, I will."

She rests her head against my shoulder. "I've been listening to "Streets of Philadelphia" again and again," she says. "What is wrong with me?"

"I told you, you're gonna be okay."

"You don't know that."

"I do. I know. You have to. I need you. Okay? I need you in my life, Winter."

"Can we get In-N-Out?" she asks. "I need a Double-Double."

We get Double-Doubles and park the car and eat on the hood, the sun setting purple over the horizon, the smog thick like soup. We're holding hands. We're soulmates. *She's gonna be all right, she's gonna be all right.* I'm repeating this like a mantra. I will say it until we hear for sure. But there's a creeping dread simmering in my belly. Because I know that nothing in my life has ever gone like it should have. I'm a master at disaster.

The last bite of the Double-Double tastes like it's gone bad.

I spit it into the hot wind.

35

• • • • •

Winter – Nico Sullivan

Mom doesn't question when I go stay at Winter's—honestly, I was becoming such a glum energy suckage, she was ready to have me out of her hair. Edina accepts it as two best friends who'd been apart getting in some bonding time. We were a couple of weeks out from school breaking for the summer, so it didn't make sense to return. I promised the 'rents I'd go back in the fall, but I was crossing my fingers at the time, and I'll be eighteen by then. School is definitely in the rearview mirror for me. So, Winter and I are basically on vacation, except for having to wait for her HIV results to come back. I swear to do everything in my power to take her mind off it, the bonus being I'll be distracted from thinking about the band and Evan. Each day, we do Winter & Nico things. Like picking peonies and leaving them by the Viper Room for River Phoenix. Joyriding in my car with the mixtape I made for when the Bouquets started touring (I'm almost finished) and singing at the top of our lungs from Letters to Cleo to the Breeders' "Cannonball". We visit LACMA for a Rothko exhibition. Movie-hop one day and see *Apollo 13* (snore), *Braveheart* (double snore, except I wouldn't say no to William Wallace in bed), and *Babe* (cute). We browse albums at the Tower Records on Sunset and buy Radiohead's *The Bends, Mellon Collie and the Infinite Sadness* by The Smashing Pumpkins, Elliot Smith (although I question the suicidal ramifications in terms of Winter's state of mind), Pavement's *Wowee Zowee*, Garbage, and The Foo Fighters, which is weird because it means Dave Grohl is moving on from Nirvana. A signal that it's time for all of us to do the same. We gorge on donuts at the Farmer's Market, eat at the Hamburger Hamlet, or Chasen's when we're feeling fancy, have brain freezes from ice cream at Thrifty's, see Dennis Woodruff driving by in his crazy car, buy some vintage 60s pieces on Melrose, and each night go to a concert: Weezer, the Dandy Warhols, White Zombie, Mad Season, the Chili Peppers, and Everclear. I keep Winter spinning around and around like a top, so she never falls. We're high most of the time, but only on good pot she gets from her guy. For the last concert, we see 311 because Jeremy has the hots for the lead singer. It's not really my kind of music, but Jeremy and Winter are super into it, and afterwards we go to Steven Spielberg's restaurant Dive in Century City and she tells Jeremy over dinner pancakes about waiting for the HIV test.

He's super quiet for a minute, and then asks: "When will you know?"

It's so late we're the only ones left in the place besides a waitress looking to leave. My pancakes have congealed to the syrupy lake of my plate. Winter shrugs.

"Probably soon. It's been almost a week."

An imaginary fork stabs me in the stomach. We've kept ourselves so busy I'd almost forgotten. But now reality has returned. Tomorrow's Friday and if we don't hear, it likely won't be till Monday. I don't know if it's better to have three more days of agony.

Now Jeremy and Winter are crying and hugging one another.

"Girl, I love you so much," Jeremy's saying. "You are my favorite person on this Earth. I've been so busy at the salon. I should've—"

"Jer, it's not you like could've stopped this from happening."

"But I—"

"No—"

"Babe, I should've—"

"I was a runaway train; nothing could've stopped me. Sometimes, I think…"

Now the imaginary fork is stabbing harder, out for blood.

"Not that I wanted it…" She twists a napkin in her fist. "But that I knew subconsciously. And I liked playing with fire."

I join them on their side of the booth, all of us wrapped up in a three-way hug. On tour, I'd forgotten about them, too caught up in my own ass. But no one in my life has ever been as important as Winter or Jeremy, not the band, not even Evan. Boys would come and go but true friendships will never leave. Unless…

I break away from them and rush to the bathroom. I'm shaking as I look in the mirror, saying a prayer to keep Winter healthy. That I would do *anything* as long as she'd be all right, give up fame, never pursue it again, whatever it took. When I return to the booth, they're paying the bill, sniffling as we head back to my car.

At Winter's, Jeremy's exhausted from the news and the pot and passes out in Winter's bed in a fetal position with Benny Bear. Winter lights some candles, and we sit by the window looking out on her front lawn.

"How are you doing?" I ask.

She bites her lip. "Tonight was a lot," she whispers. "With Jeremy and all."

"He needed to know."

She nods at that. "I'm tired, Nico," she says.

I kiss her on the forehead. "I'm gonna get some air."

I take a notebook and a pen and sit on a lawn chair outside watching sleepy Laurel Canyon at three in the morning. Barely a sound can be heard, the air a mix of smog and freshly-cut grass. I haven't written a song since the album, too out-of-sorts to put thought to paper. But it flows out of me now, as if I need to be exorcized.

Winter
I could lose you
From a mistake
You were wild
Too much to take

Thought us invincible
Strong as a wall
But we're made of glass
Shatter from a fall

Sex and blood brought us here
To a place where we fear
The final nail in the grave
To a beautiful girl, once called babe

Now poison flows through veins
And soon will come the pain
A body filled with disease
'Bout to bring us to our knees

You are Winter, untouched and white
You are Winter, my soul's delight
You are Winter, brutal and bare
You are Winter, harsh and fair

You are Winter
You are Winter
You are Winter

And now I'm cold
Left all alone
Just a black hole
An empty bowl
Without a goal
It's taken toll

On me, on me

It's taken toll

You are Winter

I start harmonizing the song, singing into the air, giving the words body, power, bringing them to life. This is for Winter *and* for what I've been through too. There's no mistaking that the breakdown of Evan and I are in the lyrics as well. "Winter" encompasses everything, all death that's touched me, even Kristen. Every heartbreak my young life has already experienced.

When I finish, I look up and see Winter by her open window, the candles flickering across her face, illuminating her in gold. She's alive, fuller than ever, far from diminished. And she will stay that way no matter the news. She will not decay. I won't let her.

She closes the window, but leaves the candles lit all through the night when I return to her bed and cuddle her close. We wake up in the morning to the phone screaming with Planned Parenthood on the other line and a test that turns out to be negative.

36

• • • • • •

Connection – Elastica

After the way-too-close call with Winter's results, I'm back at Mom's, a little less glum than before. It's as if the trauma I'd experienced moved that *other* trauma to the wayside. I mean, I'm still upset about not being on tour, or making videos, or going on MTV with Daisy Fuentes, but thinking back, did I really like all that stuff? I loved singing on stage, don't get me wrong, but the fame part made me super anxious. I think it's why I was drinking all the time, like I didn't know how to deal with it otherwise. Since I've been back, I haven't really gone downstairs to swipe from Mom's liquor cabinet. Partly because she only has shit like cherry cordial and other old lady drinks, but also because I'm not really feeling it right now. I kinda wanna make music again, in my own way. "Winter" inspired me hella bad.

On a whim, I call Terry Carbon, just for some kind of advice. My fingers dial before my brain can even say it's a bad idea. I mean, he was always the most cool with me. I'm surprised he takes my call. He's rightfully pissed at the band. He found us so he had a lot riding on our success. But he tells me that I was the star he was looking for all along and the rest of them were "accoutrement". When he asks what I've been doing, I go into the Winter saga and the song I wrote.

"Sing it for me," he says.

"Now?"

"No other time but the present."

So I sing "Winter" to him, honestly having practiced before and pretty sure how I want the melody to go. When I finish, the room sort of sparkles, like there's magic in the air. My heart beating like hella crazy.

He's silent for a second, and I think I've bombed. The song probably cheesy to him.

"Nico," he says, and I tell myself I don't care what he thinks. This song is for Winter, it's for me; who gives a shit if the rest of the world gets to hear? He clears his throat. "Let's get you in a studio."

Two days later, he's flown out and picks me up from Mom's in a rented BMW convertible. We kiss three times on the cheek like old friends.

"I got you a guitarist. Name's Kip Treemont, local kid. He's played back-up in a few of our bands' recordings."

He touches my leg, innocently. Just three pats, but he keeps his hand close, ready to squeeze the next time. Elastica's "Connection" is on the radio, and he's singing along. He has a pretty awful voice for someone so into music. Maybe his whole life is based around jealousy. He's grown a goatee and looks at me through his purple John Lennon sunglasses. I wonder if he goes to sleep in them.

"Nico, this is what you're meant to do. Solo. No one dragging you down. They were fucking dragging you down. Dimming your shine. You know when you called, I was thinking about you." He purrs, his words vibrating. "About a new record that just you would record. The execs were very pleased when I told them."

"I'm surprised they wanna work with me again, I mean after the last album flopped."

"It underperformed," he says, lighting a cigarette. "I wouldn't be here if it flopped."

His hand moved toward my leg. "I missed you."

"Yeah." I let him leave his hand, it's still innocent. He's only squeezing my thigh. The rush I felt before with the prospect of fame and success fills my belly again, takes hold. He keeps his hand there until we reach the studio where I meet Kip Treemont who looks like Slash from Guns N' Roses down to the nose ring. On a couch, we go through the song, Terry Carbon hovering like a gnat. I want to swat him away. I'm thinking about his hand on my thigh that didn't have liver spots but was still gross. He keeps winking at me like he has something in his eye. I wonder if he'll suggest a hotel room and what I'll do when he asks.

Slash—I mean, Kip Treemont, is a decent guitar player, but he's not getting the song right. He's playing it too sad, while I want it more poppy, this new alt-grunge sound that's been emerging, less needle in the arm and more tattoo on a lunch break. We go in the booth to record, but the song is not working. Terry Carbon can see it and is growing more and more frustrated with each verse. Kip is less into the groove each time we start up again. And the words are just plopping out of my mouth instead of each one shining like a golden nugget. We take a break and I go splash water on my face. When I step outside, Terry Carbon is in the hallway.

"What is it, love?" he asks, now with a stronger accent than before.

"I dunno, we're not connecting. Like, we don't have a connection."

I think of the Elastica song. And then my mind goes to the only true connection I've ever had — Evan. How if he was in the studio, we'd deliver "Winter" like a newborn baby. We'd give it life. And I miss him. I have missed him and used Winter's drama to avoid thinking about it. I've accepted the band breaking up, but not from him.

Terry Carbon gets closer, enough that I can smell the mint he placed on his tongue. "You gotta work on that connection, right? It's all about connection."

I step back. "What if I gave the song to Evan?"

He stops cold. "Who? You mean the guitar player?"

"My boyfriend," I say, baring my teeth. "I mean, he was."

"I think it's time you forget about him."

Terry Carbon uses his grubby fingers to curl a dangling hair around my ear.

"If you want this…" He's pressing against me, a slight sway to him likely from nips of liquor in the flask I saw him holding.

The hallway gets spinny. A million thoughts racing. *Don't blow this. Knee him in the balls. He can get you back on the top of the charts. I wish Evan were here.*

"Not without Evan," I murmur.

He's nuzzling my ear. "What?"

"I said, *not* without Evan." I push him, and the look on his face is one of pure surprise. Maybe I'm the only girl who's ever rebuffed him. Maybe it's finally time. I take in this small man, as he gets his bearings. The look of shock turns to hate.

"You ungrateful…"

"I'm gonna, like, stop you before you say something really messed up. I don't need you, or Grouch, or anyone really. I'll do this all myself. You watch."

I turn and walk away, imagining him stewing.

"You'll be sorry," he calls out. "You're not going anywhere without me."

"Maybe not," I yell back. "But wherever I'm going, I'll be proud of it."

I slam into the emergency exit doors as the alarm blares and the L.A. sun hits me like an explosion. He drove me here, but I'll walk home, even though no one ever walks in L.A., even if it takes miles and I have to cross highways. I'll be replaying this moment in my skull and that'll be enough to keep me occupied.

And when I get home, I'll get in my car and drive to Eugene, where I hope I'll find Evan after his walk-about's done. Whatever happens next, I can at least say that I tried.

37

• • • • •

Loser – Beck

First, I check out the apartment Evan used to rent, but find no one home. His neighbor pops out, a dude I vaguely remember being called Ramsey, who lived in his pajamas and always smelled of Cheetos. "I'm looking for Evan," I say, and point to myself. "It's Nico." He's so high he can barely keep his eyes open, the culprit being the plastic skull bong in his hand.

"Right, right, from the band. He's over at the Open Mic at Café Hey."

I rush away without even thanking him, booking it to my car and driving the few blocks to Café Hey. It's kismet, since Café Hey was where Evan and I first met. Now it would be the place where we'd reunite, written in the stars.

Café Hey smells of mocha when I walk in. There's a small crowd listening to the Open Mic. I take a seat on a frilly couch in the back, order a latte from the waitress, and put on a scarf so I fit in more with the Oregon scene. A girl is on stage reading poetry about

Sandra Day O'Connor being the first woman to oversee the Supreme Court. When she finishes, everyone claps. My latte arrives and it's warming since Eugene has the kind of permanent chill that L.A. never could. The MC jumps up on stage.

"And now I have a treat for you," he says. "Evan Marvin, guitarist from the band Grenade Bouquets, who were on *MTV's Top 20*—"

"No, man," Evan says, taking the mic from him. "Just Evan Marvin, no more band."

"Ri-ght," the MC says, and slinks off stage.

Evan looks thinner, like he hasn't had a full meal since we parted, but at the same time, he looks super healthy. He's all sinewy, so I assume his walkabout was a success. He's wearing his Docs, torn black jeans and a jean jacket tied around his waist along with a moss-green striped sweater I'd grown to love. His beard grown, tickling down his neck now, which also boasts a tiny tattoo of a grenade with the pin pulled.

"I recently came back from a walkabout," he says, stroking his beard. "Oregon's a good place for that, right? Like endless woods and woods. I camped, saw a bear, cooked a lot of beans, forgot about which day it was—it was kind of perfect. I thought I'd find a muse to write songs again, I dunno, I'm pretty disillusioned about that now. Yeah, I was on MTV, but that won't be on my tombstone. Hey, I'm a loser, baby, so why don't you kill me? Speaking of which, I figured I'd play that for you."

He launches into a glittering acoustic cover of Beck's "Loser". I never really paid attention to the song before, but this cover has heft. It makes me realize how much he blames himself for our demise, and the band's, and maybe for us as well. When he finishes, I'm tearing up into my latte and wipe them away. I have my notebook with the "Winter" song, but I'm not sure he needs to see it anymore. Maybe we'd both be better off if I left without him ever seeing me here, and the last memory I'd have of him would be his cover of "Loser".

I gather up my scarf when the waitress comes over.

"Get you another? Or a dessert?"

"What?" I'm stunned out of the loop I'd entered in my mind. The door seems so far away. "Uh, sure."

"Our apricot scones are to die," she says.

"Consider me slayed then."

She leaves and her movement catches Evan's eye. He looks over and I descend into the shadows, but we make contact. He gives the tiniest of smiles, enough to assure me it was good I stayed. He slings his guitar over his shoulder and comes over.

"Caught my little set, did ya?" he asks, sitting on the other end of the frilly couch. The waitress brings my latte and a scone.

"Can I get you anything too?" she asks him.

We stare at each other, unsure what to do. To ask for a coffee commits him to stay.

"I'll get—"

"Get something—"

We laugh and he orders a cappuccino. Neither of us knowing what to say, our eyes chasing anything else but one another.

"Hey, Café Hey looks the same," I say.

"Some things never change." His cappuccino arrives. "Like this coffee, they always make the foam into a shape of a tree."

"So, your walkabout…?"

"Yeah, it was…" He flips the hair out of his face and takes a sip. "Really cool, I mean, just me and nature getting to know one another."

"And you got a tattoo," I say, pointing to the grenade on his neck with the pin pulled.

He rubs it awkwardly. "Yeah, I dunno, I guess to remind me about the band and to live life like I'm holding a grenade with the pin pulled. Like to always only do what makes me happy."

"Yeah, I hear that."

I bite into the apricot scone, which really is to die for.

"What about you?" he asks. "Did you go home?"

"Yeah, and then Winter had this drama." His eyebrows rise. "But it turned out not to be. Still, it was scary before we knew."

"I can imagine."

"And then like I was in touch with Terry Carbon."

"That dick? Why?"

"I wrote this song and he was interested and booked me studio time."

"Really, Nico?"

"Yeah, with a guitarist and all, but it wasn't right. I mean, it didn't feel right, ya-know? And he got all handsy."

"He what?"

"It's okay, I didn't let him do anything. He was always creepy."

"Super creepy."

"And when I was singing the song and it didn't feel right with the guitarist, I couldn't help but think of you. Of us."

He sips his cappuccino, stoic as ever.

"We had something really good, Evan. And it feels like a part of me is missing without you."

He shakes his head. "Nico..."

"No, I'm not here to get you back. I mean, I dunno, I...just had to come. Like, I got in my car and drove because we left things so shitty between us."

He takes a deep breath, blows at his bangs. "Yeah, we did."

"I couldn't never see you again. Have my stay in the hospital be the last conversation we ever had. I'm sorry."

"What are you sorry about?"

I don't expect this question from him. I'm stammering until I can recalibrate.

"I...everything. Like, I was a shit. I had stars in my eyes, and I couldn't see around them. I never wanted to destroy the Bouquets."

"I know you didn't."

"Or hurt you in any way. That dude I was with...I'm so embarrassed. And I treated you so terribly. I took us for granted. I have these mood swings, always have, and maybe I need to look into that, talk to someone, or medication..."

"I don't think you need medication." He picks up his guitar and plucks at it. "You're a teenager."

"You're a teenager too!"

"I'm at the *very* end of my teen years. And I'm a loser, baby, so it doesn't even matter."

I'm kinda smiling. "I'm the loser."

"We're both losers. Don't blame yourself. We

got a taste of the wildest drugs out there: fame and fortune. They can fuck you up."

"They really did fuck me up."

"But there's more to life. More exciting things. More meaningful things than that. So, it's a learning experience, like everything."

"Very wise."

"Hey, I'm about to not be a teenager anymore, I'm wise."

He smirks and I fall in love with him all over again. I want to kiss his beard all the way down to his big toe.

"Can I give you a hug, Evan?"

He takes the guitar off his lap. "Sure."

I lean into his arms and his smells like the woods, rough and rowdy. Our hug lasts for eons. I don't want to let go, and I don't think he does either.

"Do you miss making music?" I ask, as we still embrace.

"Of course, music is my blood."

"Can I sing you the song I wrote?"

He doesn't answer immediately, and I worry I pushed too far. But then he gives a "huh, huh" laugh. "Yeah, let's take it outside."

Café Hey is near to some woods so we walk there. It's pretty idyllic: birds chirping, nary a soul. We find a felled tree and park our butts on it. He noodles on his guitar. I take out my notepad with "Winter".

"It's called 'Winter'," I say, and then I sing. After the first verse, he joins in playing and we're symbiotic again like we've never been separated. I lean into the flow of his strums, close my eyes and there's no one else I see. When the song ends, I'm breathless. I open my eyes and he's staring back in awe.

"That was something," he says, biting his cheek. I think he's afraid his grin will be too wide.

"Yeah," I say, taking deep gulps of the pure air.

I toss the notepad aside and lunge at him, knocking us over the felled tree as we rustle around in the dirt, nose to nose.

"Hi."

"Hi."

And then we kiss. Any pain we caused to each other melting away, if just for that moment. Even if it's only a spark and not meant to sustain, we'll have that moment and that is enough.

38

• • • • •

Sometimes Always – Jesus and Mary Chain

The 'rents allow me to bunk up with Evan for the immediate future, at least for the summer. How could they deny love? We fall into a groove. Sleeping in, him making breakfast, reading through his collection of Dostoevsky, coffees at Café Hey, limited pot and alcohol because as cheesy as it is, we're too high on each other. Music we keep at a distance. We slowly start to listen again to favorites. Deep cuts of Nirvana, Hole's first album, early Smashing Pumpkins like *Gish*, Mudhoney and Nine Inch Nails, Folk Implosion's "Natural One", PJ Harvey's slinky and seductive "Down by the Water", and then lighter fare like Belly and Juliana Hatfield, Better Than Ezra, Weezer and Oasis, the new kings of the charts, and Jesus and Mary Chain. Somehow, we're listening to a lot of Jesus and Mary Chain.

My notebook stays closed, ever since that one time I sang "Winter" in the woods to him. We don't want to tempt fate. Music brought us together but destroyed us as well, and neither wants to be the one to make the same mistake twice. We take walks in the woods, we forage for berries, we brew outrageous teas, we never turn on the television. We smoke cigarettes in the nude on his fire escape late at night. The time I climbed up that fire escape to the roof where I almost leaped off feels like centuries ago.

We take home a lost cat. He's a skinny thing, grey, but when we give him a bath, he's almost white. We call him Dave Grohl. Dave Grohl is skittish at first, hiding under the bed for most of the day. At night, he begins to lurk and soon decides he likes my lap. We get him checked at the vet and make sure he has all his shots. We feel like a little family. Summer comes and with it the Oregon heat. It's not raining anymore. But a hundred degrees in Eugene is still a nice day so we purchase bikes and mine has a basket where we put Dave Grohl and explore the town. It's full of college students who stayed, and I wonder what it might be like to go there with him. What would I major in? Maybe English Literature? Read a lot of the Brontë sisters. Minor in a theater where I'd act in a play. It seems carved out of someone else's life, hard to find the groove to make it fit.

We start going to see local bands. Honey Pot, The Flaggs, Machines Like Us, Soft. There are less mosh pits than there used to be. It's more shoegazing. After one show, Soft covers Jesus and Mary Chain's "Sometimes Always" and we think that's funny because we'd just been listening to that song. On a walk afterwards, I'm singing.

"Aw you're a lucky son

Lucky son of a gun
You went away, you went away
You went away but now you're back."

The song telling, a summation of us and the trials we went through to get back together. He takes my hand and there's so much energy passing through our palms I almost faint. If he would've asked me to marry right there, I would've said yes.

"Come," I say, leading him home, because I want to make beautiful music with him.

We light the candles dripping all over the floor. We open the windows wide. He kicks off his Docs and loses his shirt, grabs his guitar and starts plucking. I know exactly where I left my notepad and unearth it. "Winter" stares back, ready to be given life. He's playing a variation of "Sometimes Always". Slowly, it morphs into a brand-new creation. He has recording equipment and two microphones. I aim one at his guitar and bring the other to my lips as "Winter" is born.

We make love afterwards, forgetting about what occurred, but in the morning a fresh cassette waits to be listened. We're salivating to hear how it sounds. Evan puts it in the boombox, presses play. The tiny apartment fills with our new child. It sounds better than anything we've ever done. It sounds like two people who've been making music together for years. His hand is shaking as he stops the tape.

"Whoa," he says.

"Yeah."

"That's really good. I mean, *really* really good."

"What should we do?" I ask, getting excited, seeing a pathway unfold with Evan and I touring together, sticking our middle finger up at the rest of the Bouquets, and Terry Carbon, and Grouch Records.

"What do you mean, what should we do?" he asks, concerned, a line forming between his eyes.

"Well, Terry Carbon's out, but I'm sure we can get another record company to listen."

"Yeah, no."

I start tickling him but he's not into it. "What do you mean, no?"

He picks me up off of him and places me to the side. "I mean, no. As is no. I don't want this to go to a record company."

"Oh. Well, then what...?"

He snaps, "It's for me. And you. Me and you, Nico. I want to be with you—"

"I wanna be with you too—"

"And make music together..."

I'm nodding like crazy.

"*But* just for us. Like that's all that matters. Right?"

"I...it's just, that song is so good. We have a chance—"

"We have a chance for a real relationship and everything that could come with it. Marriage, kids down the road. But we can't be in a real band together. It'll only end all fucked up."

"No, Grenade Bouquets got all fucked up because of Ed and Randy and Lacey—"

"And me. And you, Nico. We're just as much to blame as them. And it's gonna happen again."

"Who says?"

"It's the way things are. Look at any relationships in bands. Like Fleetwood Mac, or Sonny and Cher."

"Those were so long ago. Things are different now."

"Kurt Cobain and Courtney Love."

Ouch.

"I don't want to tempt fate," he says. "And I want you to really think about what you want. If you to be in a successful band and make music and that be your life, I don't want to get in the way."

"You'd never get in the way."

"Listen to me, Nico, this last month has been awesome. We've gotten along so well, and it's because we haven't let music be the third person in the relationship. That's why. I-I've been meaning to tell you this, but I have to go home for a bit. It's my brother Chris."

"What's wrong?"

"He's not doing well at the facility he's in, so my dad wants to get him into a better one. I need to help him move to a new place. He doesn't deal with change well."

"I could come!" I say, because the thought of being without him is too hard to process.

"I'd love to have you meet my family, but not this way. It's gonna be a rough time. I want to shield you from that."

"I can handle it."

"I know you can, but it'll stress me out more to have you there. I need to focus on Chris, and maybe it's a good time for you to figure out what you want too."

I pull away from him, hugging my flannel close like a security blanket. "Are you breaking up with me?"

"No, Nico. Definitely not." He strokes my arms. "But I think we really do need to figure out where we're headed. Because I want to play music too, but not in the limelight, just as something we do because we love it. I can't chase the fame again with you and go through everything we did."

"What if we're together and play music but like locally in Café Hey, and other places like that? It's not like there's other record executives knocking down our doors, right? So that's only a pipe dream anyway. It's stupid to even think about."

He wraps his arms around me. "I would love to do a set with you at Café Hey as boyfriend and girlfriend. I can't think of a better way to spend my time."

I tell myself this is what I want. That he is more important than anything else. And that we'll still get to make music, on our own terms. I tell myself that this is enough and always will be.

"What should we call ourselves then?" I ask, looking up into his blue eyes as he lightly swings me.

"How about Evanico? Simple as that."

I let it dance on my tongue. "Evanico. I like it."

"And thus, on our lord's day of July the 22nd and the year nineteen hundred and ninety-five, Evanico was born."

39

• • • • •

Rock Star – Hole

For my eighteenth birthday, Winter and Jeremy take me to a club inspired by the Scream painting with a staircase that's like a descent to hell. We wear stickers that a blacklight would pick up, and dance around to a punk band that gives off Rancid vibes. Evan's in Idaho helping his brother get into a new facility and from what I hear it's not going well. School starts up in a few weeks and I tell the 'rents I'm gonna return, but I'm not. I'll likely head back to Eugene to live with Evan where we can play local bars and maybe I could wait tables, or... I could try to record an album. I'd been penning my thoughts in my notepad recently, reams of songs that are actually hella good. I haven't put them to music yet, or even told him about it. There's part of me that wonders if I'm too damn young to give up on being a rock star and play housewife. And honestly, I don't think that's what Evan really wants either. He just doesn't want to admit that we could have it all: the love and the fame.

After a bout of wild dancing in the dark (he, he), I convene with Winter and Jeremy by the bar. My Sasha Lioni fake ID gets us fireballs from a bartender with foot-long spikes in her hair. She's dreamy.

"So, have you decided yet?" Winter yells over a new group raging on the stage.

"What?" I shout back.

"Girl, with what you're gonna do?" Jeremy asks.

"I wanna be with Evan," I say, wiping the cinnamon burn from my lips after a shot.

"And give up being Nico the Star?" Winter asks.

"I was hardly a star," I say.

"Uh, I have the magazine clippings to prove it," Jeremy says. "They'll be other boys than what's-his-name, men even. You're eighteen now, you can date anyone!"

We see an older dude with an exaggerated mustache and a leather jacket with studs eyeing us.

"Gross," I say, pushing Jeremy away. "Anyway, what's the point of staying here? You'll be at the Sassoon Academy in Santa Monica."

"Santa Monica is L.A.!"

"Santa Monica is the West side," I say. "So far."

He burps in my ear. "It's forty-five minutes."

"Without traffic, which is never."

"Fine never visit me, never see me again."

Jeremy's dancing in place. He's wearing a white jacket with pins and baggy jeans, his hair frosted blond now, the tips ultra-frosted.

"You're gonna be so busy with all the men hitting on you," Winter says. "Like the opposite of high school. Everyone there is gay."

"Yes, I plan on orgies." We all squeal. "You two can't have all the fun."

"What fun?" Winter asks, pushing her rainbow sunglasses up into her nest of hair. She's lost the dreds, but it's still colored bone-white. She's wearing a plaid skirt with a top that's not a bra but might as well be a bra. "I've been dodging AIDS and pages from my two old dudes."

"Don is still hitting you up?" I ask, dumbfounded.

"It's mostly Zedd. He doesn't have *it* by the way. And yeah, Don still pages me on my beeper. Does he think I have a death wish? But it's not like there's anyone else."

"Winter, you didn't—" I begin to say.

"No, Nico, I never even entertained. I keep his dick hanging. Don't worry, I won't be going into crisis again anytime soon." She gives me a wet willie. "So, you've decided on love over success?"

"It's not like success is a guarantee. I have no contract. My old record company won't have anything to do with me. We've long been falling down the charts. I'm surprised anyone remembers us."

Jeremy hugs my belly. "We'll always remember you, Nico Nicotine."

"And I will still be singing and making music. Evan and I even have a band name. Evanico."

Jeremy and Winter give stank faces. "Are you sticking with that?" they both say and the same time and then lock hands and screech.

"I think it's cute," I say, and I picture us playing at Café Hey while college kids sip on their lattes. A far cry from stadiums. "As long as we'll be together."

The band on stage cover Hole's "Rock Star", and

Winter and Jeremy screech again and jump up and down.

"Come, Nico, let's dance," they call out.

"I want a cigarette."

"You can have one in here," Winter says.

"I want some air."

"Whatever," they say, giving me the *Clueless* W with their fingers. We'd just seen it at the Egyptian Theater and have been quoting it like hella "as if".

I give them deuces and head outside to an alleyway. Lighting my cigarette, I'm telling myself over and over how happy I'll be with Evan, even though there's a massive part of my heart that wants to be on a real stage, with rabid fans, touching someone's soul with my song. Signing autographs until I get carpel tunnel. Could I ever be really happy without that? I start to sing to the night:

" *You are Winter, untouched and white*
You are Winter, my soul's delight
You are Winter, brutal and bare
You are Winter, harsh and fair."

"Could I bum one?" I hear a voice ask.

I take in a white baby doll dress, white stockings and pale knees. As I pan upwards, goosebumps break out along my arms. The red, red lips, the dyed blonde-white hair, the deer-in-headlights eyes. My nemesis turned idol, Courtney Love, who I once hated out of jealousy and now adore.

"Uh…"

"Liked the song too," she says, as I hold out the cigarette pack and she flips one into her lips, lights it and smokes out of the side of her mouth. " *You are Winter,*" she sings.

"Uh…"

"Is that all you can say?" she asks and shows all of her teeth as she laughs. Her front tooth has a dab of lipstick—she's so human.

"I-I'm a big fan."

She waves the smoke away from me. "Stop."

"No, I…" I'm about to tell her my whole saga. How last year I ran away from home to show up at Kurt Cobain's door. But she doesn't want to hear about her dead husband. She's had enough of that. I just watched a Barbara Walters' interview where Courtney Love told a story about yelling at Kurt for dropping the baby and how she thinks it's one of the reasons he killed himself. Because they were always civil to one another and she was mean that day.

"I've covered your song," I say instead, trying to be cool. It's not like my stomach isn't on fire, but I focus on smoking my cig, on not fainting.

"Oh yeah? Like that band?" She jerks her thumb back at the club.

"'Violet'," I say. "It's how we got noticed. Well, before—"

"So, you're noticed." She squints her eyes, observes me up and down, takes a long drag. "Yeah, I know you."

I'm turning red. "No, you don't."

"Yeah, yeah I fucking know you. Your video. The… uh…Grenades, right? Bad ass."

My body goes numb. "Grenade Bouquets."

"Right, Bouquets, yeah. I love anything where a chick is in charge and the dudes are in the back."

"I can die right now," I say, and then clamp my hand over my mouth. "I'm sorry, I didn't mean… I don't know, this is all surreal."

"Calm your tits down," she says, finishing the cigarette. "You got another?"

"Sure." I pass one over and she lights it.

"My only vice now, right? I gotta be good."

"What are you... What are you doing here?"

She looks around as if she doesn't realize where she
is. "Here, like, here? Or on this planet." She cackles.
"Don't really have the answer to either. Floating, I
guess. Making bad choices."

I know one of her bandmates died of an overdose.
That she was arrested twice and is being sued by two
concertgoers who said she struck them during a show.
She's smaller than I thought she would be, less of a
presence, more real, more broken—that's if she really
is here and not just a figment of my imagination.

"We're playing a show in Irvine tomorrow," she
says, scratching her arm. "I'm taking a break from my
band and I don't know, seeing some live music, going
where the wind takes me. You on tour?"

I look down at my shoes, as if I'm embarrassed.
"We...broke up."

She points her cigarette at me. "Lemme guess, those
fuckers couldn't deal with you in the spotlight?"

"It's more complicated than that, but yeah."

"What were you singing just now?"

"Oh, a song I wrote. It's about my friend who
thought she had HIV. But it's about the death of a
lot of things: relationships, people. I've had a lot of it
recently. I-I don't have to tell you."

She digs a knuckle into her eye. "You're angry,
aren't you?"

"My sister died suddenly." I almost choke on a breath. "And yeah, I used to be. I was all anger. I couldn't escape it."

"I scream his name at shows, I'm so goddamn angry." She clenches her fists. "KURT," she screams, tipping her head back. "I act out his death. I keep his ashes and some of his hair in a Buddhist shrine. Don't ask me what helps, 'cause I don't know."

I'm not only crying now, I'm weeping. "He was… beautiful."

She gives a cig a good suck. "Yeah, well, he's gone. All we have left in life of them are memories. It's cruel. I used to sleep in bed with his mom because they kinda were the same size. It was like he was there, sometimes, in the morning when I'm still attached to my dreams. He doesn't visit like he used to."

"Neither does Kristen." Courtney Love looks at me screwy. "My sister. She used to—"

"They have better things to do, right. Bocce with God or something. I dunno. They say I have a death wish, but I think I'll live to ninety-five. I'll show them all." She nods to her cigarette. "Unless these finish me off of course." She ashes it on the bottom of her heel. "So, no more Grenades, what's next?"

"Our record company were assholes." She laughs at that. "And like recently a guy there tried to make a pass at me."

"Ugh, men. I'd love to weed wacker some of their schlongs."

"So, I'm not sure. I'm still with the guitarist, we're together. He wasn't into the fame part, but I've been writing these new songs and really do want to record them."

"You should. There are a million record companies. And you guys were good. You have a voice."

I'm gushing. "I can't believe you're saying that. I think you're so... I sound so dumb."

"Yeah, yeah, give me your hand. What's your name, Grenade Girl?"

"Nico, Nico Sullivan."

"Okay, Nico." She takes out a tube of lipstick and pops off the cap, starts scribbling red on my palm and down my arm. "These are my guys' info at DGC. You can send them your song."

"Wow, you don't have to—"

She looks me dead in the eyes. "I know I don't, but I am. Stop apologizing for yourself so much. Fucking girls are always told to apologize for everything. Never be sorry. Do whatever you want. And lose anyone who thinks otherwise."

She finishes writing and I stare in awe at my lipstick-stained arm.

"All right, this girl's gonna turn into a pumpkin if she doesn't get a bed. We've done like a hundred shows and I couldn't tell you what day it is, but you're an angel, don't let anyone tell you're not, and blow shit up even more than you already have."

I mime an explosion as she gives a drunken half wave and clomps back into the club. Once she's gone, I quickly glance down at my arm to make sure her lipstick is actually there, and this had not been my wild imagination, but an oracle telling me exactly what my soul needed to do.

40

• • • • •

BONUS TRACK
Blow Up the Outside World – Soundgarden

In a month it'll be the second anniversary of Kristen's death—hard to believe. I haven't visited her grave since last summer. I bring a bottle of wine and two plastic glasses, so we can toast. Of course, I have the mixtape I made from when the Bouquets first went on tour culminating when I shared cigarettes with Courtney Love in an alleyway.

"Hey, Kelly," I say, referring to Kelly Taylor from *90210*. Kristen was shiny Kelly, and I was Brenda, surly fuckin' Brenda. It's a joke we had for years, defining our sisterhood. "Been a while." I pour some red for her and for me. "Cheers, girl." I take an indulging sip. "I made you another mixtape." I leave the tape on the tombstone next to the last one I made for her. "I think you'll like this more. It's less empty-a-vein grunge, and more...well, not pop, but poppier, I guess. I'm sure you saw what I've been up to. Yeah, I had a hit album for a sec and a video climbing the MTV charts. It was all hella cool until it wasn't. But I've been writing again, and I'm trying to decide what my next step will be. If you were still alive, you'd be in college probably on a track scholarship, doing pre-MD, busy as hell, but happy, I know you'd be happy. I'm trying to find that happiness too. And singing really did that for me. Evan did too. I told you about him the last time, but now we've been together for over a year, minus a break-up in the middle. He was in Idaho for a bit helping out his brother, but he just got back to Oregon and wants me to live with him. I know, I know, it's crazy to think Mom and Dad would let this happen, but I'm eighteen now, just turned, and there's really nothing they can do. I think they've given up trying to box me in. And school, well, school was never for me as you can remember, but singing… I feel like I'm doing something special. Here's the prob, though. Evan doesn't want to be famous, meaning I gotta choose between him or being a rock star. And that's the bind I'm in. I love him, Kell, I really do. He makes me feel like I'm the most important person in his world, and he's kind, and beautiful, and so talented, and I think we could really be happy. But. Would I always wonder what more I could have?" I run my fingers over Kristen's name on the tombstone, bringing them to my lips while I squeeze in the tears. "So, here's what happened. I met Courtney Love and she gave me the info where to send my new single. It's called 'Winter" but it's about you too. It's about everything I've lost and have the potential to lose. I think it really has a shot to become something big." I take out a padded envelope from my purse with the tape. "So here it is, Kell, what do you think I should do? I could send it and maybe nothing happens. Evan wouldn't have to know, and we can make quiet music together in Eugene. Or maybe her big label signs us and we'll open for Hole, and then how could he say no, right? Because I think he's being so defiant because he's afraid of failing again, but we wouldn't this time. We'd be strong together. We'd defy the naysayers." I take a sip and clink her glass. "So, I'm gonna wait here for a sign. I know how much you loved Ace of Motherfuckin' Base and that song, so that will be my decider. A sign from you. I can wait all day, Kelly."

I tuck my knees up to my chin because it's a little cool for L.A. There's a wind blowing the grass on her tombstone. Is it her? I let it be her. Wiping away the tears, a chill in my bones, hella alert for that sign. The envelope sits beside me and then the wind picks it up and blows it a few feet away. I get up to chase, scoop it up and hold it close to my chest.

"I love you," I say, blowing a kiss back at her grave.

I drive out of the graveyard until I pass a mailbox on the street. My knees are knocking into one another as I step out. I'm clutching the envelope so hard that my fingers are going numb. It already has postage as if I knew what I was gonna do and didn't even need the wind or a sign from my Kelly specter, my lovely sis.

I open the mailbox and shove it inside before I can change my mind. Getting back in the car, I turn on the radio and "Blow Up the Outside World" by Soundgarden blares. Singing at the top of my lungs, I floor the gas, heading out of L.A. back to Eugene and Evan.

He'd gotten a tattoo of a grenade with the pin pulled.

That has to mean something.

I'm gonna take it as another sign because I've always lived my life like I'm about explode and wanna make the most of those final seconds.

I'm not about to stop now.

Or ever.

Four, three, two, one...

ACKNOWLEDGMENTS
· · · · ·

Huge thanks to everyone who helped bring Grenade Bouquets to life. Thank you to everyone at Wise Wolf Books for the time and dedication they put into this book. Rachel Del Grosso, for publishing this tale, along with Lauren Bridges, Kristin Yahner, and Tracey Govender for her steller edits. Nat Kimber at The Rights Factory for being an amazing agent that believed in these books. Kat Bedrosian and Dani Grammerstorf-French, for their early eyes and notes, and Mom and Dad for always supporting. And biggest thanks to all the grunge and alt bands and folk artists that became the mixtape for each chapter: Matthew Sweet, Letters to Cleo, Frente!, Hole, Sheryl Crow, Mad Season, Nine Inch Nails, Stone Temple Pilots, Freedy Johnston, Joni Mitchell, The Cranberries, Nirvana, Sunny Day Real Estate, Silverchair, Radiohead, Smashing Pumpkins, Urge Overkill, Soul Asylum, Bush, Live, Tori Amos, L7, Alice in Chains, The Breeders, Bruce Springsteen, Elastica, Beck, Soundgarden, Jesus and Mary Chain, and the biggest thanks for her inspiration, Courtney Love.

ABOUT THE AUTHOR

• • • • •

Lee Matthew Goldberg is the author of the novels THE ANCESTOR, THE MENTOR, THE DESIRE CARD, SLOW DOWN and ORANGE CITY. He has been published in multiple languages and nominated for the 2018 Prix du Polar. After graduating with an MFA from the New School, his writing has also appeared in The Millions, Vol. 1 Brooklyn, LitReactor, Monkeybicycle, Fiction Writers Review, Cagibi, Necessary Fiction, the anthology Dirty Boulevard, The Montreal Review, The Adirondack Review, The New Plains Review, Underwood Press and others.

He is the editor-in-chief and co-founder of Fringe, dedicated to publishing fiction that's outside-of-the-box. His pilots and screenplays have been finalists in Script Pipeline, Book Pipeline, Stage 32, We Screenplay, the New York Screenplay, Screencraft, and the Hollywood Screenplay contests. He is the co-curator of The Guerrilla Lit Reading Series and lives in New York City. RUNAWAY TRAIN and its sequel, GRENADE BOUQUETS are his first Young Adult novels.

CPSIA information can be obtained
at www.ICGtesting.com
Printed in the USA
LVHW030609290721
694025LV00006B/262

9 781953 944078